STILL

JOANNA COCKERLINE

Copyright © 2025 Joanna Cockerline

All rights reserved. No part of this work may be reproduced or used in any form, except brief passages in reviews, without prior written permission of the publisher.

Edited by Jeremy Luke Hill
Cover image by Bit-sinna
Book design by Jeremy Luke Hill
Set in Linux Libertine and Acumin Variable
Printed on Coach House Laid
Printed and bound by Arkay Design and Print

LIBRARY AND ARCHIVES CANADA CATALOGUING IN PUBLICATION

Title: Still / Joanna Cockerline.
Names: Cockerline, Joanna, author.
Identifiers: Canadiana (print) 20250219840 | Canadiana (ebook) 20250225654 | ISBN 9781774221709 (softcover) | ISBN 9781774221723 (EPUB) | ISBN 9781774221716 (PDF)
Subjects: LCGFT: Social problem fiction. | LCGFT: Novels.
Classification: LCC PS8605.O27 S75 2025 | DDC C813/.6—dc23

ONTARIO ARTS COUNCIL
CONSEIL DES ARTS DE L'ONTARIO
an Ontario government agency
un organisme du gouvernement de l'Ontario

Canada Council for the Arts | Conseil des arts du Canada

ONTARIO CREATES | ONTARIO CRÉATIF

The Porcupine's Quill gratefully acknowledges the support of the Canada Council for the Arts, the Ontario Arts Council, and the Ontario Book Publishing Tax Credit.

The Porcupine's Quill respectfully acknowledges the ancestral homelands of the Attawandaron, Anishinaabe, Haudenosaunee, and Métis Peoples, and recognizes that we are situated on Treaty 3 territory, the traditional territory of Mississaugas of the Credit First Nation.

The Porcupine's Quill also recognizes and supports the diverse persons who make up its community, regardless of race, age, culture, ability, ethnicity, nationality, gender identity and expression, sexual orientation, marital status, religious affiliation, and socioeconomic status.

The Porcupine's Quill
130 Dublin Street North
Guelph, Ontario, Canada
N1H 4N4
www.porcupinesquill.ca

For Tasha, Tanisha, Ivy, Jessica, Jasmine, and Dee
and many more who know, or knew, these streets

For those who continue to walk,
wherever you are

And for George and Sam

To love. To be loved. To never forget your own insignificance. To never get used to the unspeakable violence and the vulgar disparity of life around you. To seek joy in the saddest places. To pursue beauty to its lair. To never simplify what is complicated or complicate what is simple. To respect strength, never power. Above all, to watch. To try and understand. To never look away. And never, never to forget.

— Arundhati Roy

Leon Avenue, Downtown Kelowna, BC
Friday, 9:00 p.m.

The night Little Zoe disappeared Kayla had been working Leon Avenue, the skies seeming starless. Cars trickled by—some people going about their business, some there to look, some more than looking.

The street was quiet in the February cold. The neon OPEN sign of the pub hummed, only the E lit. The usual people were scattered down the street, smoking or talking to themselves. Someone's radio, on the sidewalk beside their sleeping bag, emptied into the night. Streetlights hung their heads, casting triangles of light.

A man pulled up in a dirty Ford pickup. Kayla strode over, the heels of her boots grinding grit. Seven months in, this life was part survival, part dare to herself.

"How much?"

She figured this would be just another quick date—not the first of the night and not the last—but leaning towards the truck's open window, she caught a hint of a smell she'd once known: horses and hay and dusty sunlight, the mulchy depth of a barn. She felt a stab of memory.

Her eyes took it all in, the way she had trained herself to do. The truck had more than a few days of fast-food wrappers and coffee cups on the floor, along with empties of Labatt 50. On the passenger seat, along with a jar of peanut butter and a knife licked clean, lay a nail puller and a rasp, glinting under the streetlight—farrier tools for shoeing horses. Like many things, they could become weapons. But there was that hint of a barn.

"Let's go to City Park," she told him, pointing up the street towards the lake. She preferred to work in the parking lot there. It was close and efficient, and if she ever got into trouble, she had the whole street community nearby.

By day, people walked their dogs there, took selfies by the lake with the backdrop of sloping green mountains; summers it brimmed with picnicking families, ice-cream-dribbled kids toting inflatables. But on this night the only sign of a person was the swell of a sleeping bag under a tree and a brimming shopping cart.

"Oh Miss," the man said when they stopped, a touch of country in his voice.

She put her face on his shoulder, just for a moment, to breathe in that scent of a farm. From the way he moved towards her, he may have thought that feeling was for him. But she just did her job, he did his. She would save the memory of that farm smell for later.

Looking back, trying to recall any detail about Little Zoe's disappearance, she remembered only the vividness of that smell, how even the hint of a scent could transport you somewhere you thought you'd left for good, remind you of dreams you once had, the things you had done, of who you once were, or could have been.

Of who you were, now.

Later, alone in her sleeping bag on the sidewalk, looking up at the sky, the stars so hard and bright, she breathed in her hands, seeking out any trace of the farm. She at once hoped for a hint of what she had once loved, and, at the same time, was afraid she might find it.

*

To a passing car—maybe a visitor confused by the one-way streets, who didn't know this wasn't where they wanted to be—that stretch of Leon Avenue wouldn't look like much come morning. On the corner was Boyd's Autobody, windows long since boarded up, lined with a few shopping carts covered in tarps, their owners under blankets beside them. Signs for NEW CONDOS – COMING SOON were plastered over the graffiti on its walls. Between mounds of snow that had melted and frozen, melted and frozen, were patches of sidewalk, with their blackened gum and their stains and their stories.

From where she lay in her sleeping bag, Kayla watched the street come alive. Before the commuters and the traffic, the dog walkers and the shoppers, and bylaw in their SUVs, the street belonged to the people who slept along Leon Avenue, belonged to those who owned nothing else.

"Morning, darlin'." Mama B emerged from her tent, a blanket wrapped around her shoulders. Her grey hair hung in strings.

Mama B had been out here as long as anyone could remember, preferring her independence to a shelter. She felt that if you were sleeping rough, Kelowna was a decent place. She missed the room she'd rented in Vancouver's downtown east side, with its hot plate and its mattress. Its roof. But here the pace was slower, the summers warmer, and the street family she had adopted was close. She called Kelowna her retirement home—although, according to her drug charges, she wasn't quite retired.

"How you doing, Kayla? Want some tea?"

Along with her kettle, Mama B had liberated a heater and generator from Home Depot to warm the tent she shared with whomever needed a place for a time. She offered tea to folks on the street every morning, was the first to find a coat or shoes for someone who was without. She had spoken only once of the daughter she had birthed, talking on a night when both the stars and the drugs had been strong, but she answered only to Mama, and called herself by no other name.

"I'd love some tea, if it's not too much trouble," Kayla said.

"Never too much trouble for you." Mama B ducked into her tent to start the kettle.

In the pale morning light, a few people stood around, their shadows long and slanted, breath hanging in clouds. Under layers of coats, and baseball caps with hoodies pulled over top, it wasn't always easy to tell who they were, but Kayla knew—though how much depended on who was asking and why.

Over there was Lily, whose name had once been Li-Mei. Lily was stepping out of the snow pants she wore until it was time to work. Underneath she wore last night's miniskirt. She smoothed it and fished around in her giant purse, took out a pair of high-heeled boots, shoved the snow pants into her bag. Then she strode up Leon, thin legs reddening in the cold. Commuters would be on their way to work. Lily was too.

"Tea's ready, hon," Mama B called over.

Kayla extracted herself from her sleeping bag, ignoring her bad leg.

The snows had curled in mean and early that year. The usual shelters were full, and the emergency shelters were too. When Kayla first came into town last August, seven months and a lifetime ago, she had tried bedding down in the shelter. She'd used her backpack as a pillow—the only way your stuff wouldn't get stolen. But that was only one reason to sleep light, if you were a girl. No, if you slept in there, you'd never sleep through the night—not that Kayla ever did anywhere, now—and there would be that sour smell that clung to you long after you'd gone outside. Or perhaps it was more of a feeling. She preferred it out here, the stars for company. Some nights were so cold it hurt to breathe, until the stinging cold gave way to numbness.

Sipping her tea, she took her phone from her pocket. *Morning, Beautiful. Where did you end up?* Kayla texted Little Zoe. She hadn't seen her friend at the end of the night. Though Kayla and her friends worked together, tried to keep track of the licence plates of the cars they got into, the nights sometimes took their own turns.

And mornings out here had their own rhythm. Past the silhouettes of trees in City Park down the street, and across Lake Okanagan, the lights of West Kelowna shimmered quietly. Old Nelson (who wasn't actually so old in chronological years) was staring toward the mountains as he did each morning, quiet with memories. Derek was bent over his notebook, writing away, building worlds or losing himself; he had his fishing hat on, so Kayla knew his ideas must be flowing good and fast. The cowboy-hatted man with the baby trailer attached to his bike came by, rooting through the bins, bagging empty cans and bottles for recycling. The sounds still woke her some mornings. She was glad to be awake before bylaw came by on their morning rounds, to clean up the city of its refuse. And the people it considered refuse.

*

Days out here began early. There were things to get done, plans to be made. Needs to secure. Everyone was running a hustle.

Take Tyler over there, now just a heap under blankets. He had a variation of the same story every day: he'd come to town for work, but the job had dried up, and now he needed bus fare to get back home. Could you spare a dollar or two just to help him get back to his dad in Chilliwack? Sometimes it was Vancouver, other times parts further east.

Over there was Kori, leaning against the wall of the nightclub and smoking with early morning bravado. She was eyeing folks getting rounded up by bylaw, hovering like a vulture, waiting in case those sleeping outside the shelter got hauled away. Sometimes the things they couldn't keep became hers for the taking. She had a business in resale.

There was Jason with his pit bull and his BMX. He was a dealer, always full of ideas. He was the first to set up a GoFundMe account every time someone died, since grief now seemed remittable. He took a cut. He offered other services, too—getting done what needed to get done. He was up early, clearly something on the go already, or left over from the night before. Perhaps for him it was still the night before.

The common currency out here was survival.

Less easy to see, but very much present, were the kindnesses: the way the women would tell the outreach volunteers, *No, save that coat for Sally down there, she needs it more,* pointing to a new girl who had arrived in town with just boots, a miniskirt, and dreams that were not yet disillusioned. The way Dan-o the Piano Man would play you a song on the piano in the park, any song you wanted. The way Nelson would salvage something special, fix something broken, if he knew it was what you needed. The way Gloria, a Syilx woman who had been thrust into residential school as a child, looked out for the younger Indigenous girls. The way James, who had a van to live in, would welcome you inside on the coldest days and crank the heat, even though he rarely had enough money for gas. The way Lily shared the beautiful songs she sang. The way Mel shared her blanket with her dog as they sat on the sidewalk, covering him up more than herself. The way Derek would include you in a story in his notebook on a day you needed to be seen. The way Ketchum would use his hands for both comfort and violence if someone did you wrong. The way Little Zoe would lend you what she had if you were without—lipstick, lube, a dose of strength.

And Little Zoe would lend her phone sometimes too—perhaps that was all that had happened. But after not seeing her friend the day after a night of work, an unanswered message, and then another and another, Kayla couldn't help but feel uneasy.

*

Recalling the last night she saw Little Zoe, Kayla tried to remember every detail. Had she noticed anything or anyone suspicious? Maybe the old man in the Camry, with glasses from another era, who had pushed Kayla's head hard as she went down on him? What about the man who was disappointed that Kayla didn't do drugs and wouldn't use first to test if his batch was safe? Was there anything? She wanted to think, yes, if only to have something to go on, something she could unravel and hold in her hands. *This was how it happened.*

If anything had happened at all.

Anything was possible out here.

The man in the Camry had seemed a bit guilty, but maybe only towards a wife left back at assisted living, or a pension cheque that could have been differently spent. And Little Zoe wouldn't have stayed in a car if a situation was going truly south—she knew when and how to leave. She had taught Kayla that. *Always know when it's time to go.*

The ham-faced man in the minivan hadn't given her a bad feeling. Same with the turbaned farm manager in the rusted pickup. The teenager in his parents' Audi who might have been on a dare (whether from friends or himself, Kayla wasn't sure). The quiet woman who was curious to finally be with a girl. The big guy who just wanted someone to hold him in the night.

Kayla wanted to think that she would have felt something the moment anything happened to Little Zoe. And wouldn't she also feel a surge of happiness, share that rush of freedom, if Little Zoe had started a new life, if such a thing were possible? But if she'd done that, why wouldn't she have told Kayla?

Yet it had seemed just an ordinary night, Kayla doing what she did. Except for that one unexpected, complicated scent: a hint of a farm and horses and dusty sunlight, deep with memory and all it could be.

Saturday, 7:00 p.m.

"Alright, you can go in," the guy working the back door of Hearthstone Shelter said to Kayla. She didn't live there, so she wasn't supposed to be there, but some staff would bend the rules. She'd helped calm someone once when they really needed calming, and now the shelter workers quietly ignored her presence. And she didn't draw attention to herself—beyond what she had learned to do, working. Ever since she was a girl, she'd known how to stay quiet. Raising her own voice was sometimes the hard part. But she was learning out here.

Past the shelter's storage area where some folks kept their bikes, in the large room filled with bunks and people, Cerise was doing her makeup on the bed.

"Hey." Kayla looked at the bed beside Cerise's. Little Zoe's. It was made. "She's gone already?"

"Never came back last night."

Kayla stared at her friend's empty bed. Little Zoe's satin duvet was different from the usual well-used sleeping bags, stained hotel castoffs, and moth-eaten donations that covered most of the other bunks. Someone had no doubt given her those covers in the way people liked to give Little Zoe gifts. Her satin pillow was topped with a stuffed unicorn and matted plush platypus. Her gold skirt hung on a hanger duct-taped to the wall. A locker mirror and a picture of a mountain sunrise were there too—what she called her window. Taped on the wall were sketches Tyler had made her—dragons and skulls, plus designs for her next tattoo, a symbol of strength she wanted just below her shoulder. The plastic bin that held her belongings was tucked under the bed along with the jewellery box Nelson had salvaged from a dumpster. Everything was neat and tidy, how Little Zoe liked it, the same as always.

"Where is she?"

Kayla sat on Little Zoe's bed. She could smell a hint of the perfume that Little Zoe spritzed on at the drugstore every night before work. She had a favourite kind, wanted no one else to use it so that clients would associate the scent only with her.

"No idea."

Little Zoe could have scored a good date who kept her at a hotel overnight, or perhaps someone let her stay at their place. Maybe her phone had just died. Or maybe she had a paying gig that kept lasting. Little Zoe got lucky like that. Little Zoe made herself lucky like that.

Kayla took off her mittens and rubbed her hands in the shelter's welcome warmth. She looked around the room. Some people snored openly; some were curled up tight and fetal. Others cradled their phones or were moving to the music in their earbuds. There was Dan-o with his mickey and his guitar. Derek had his notebook. There was the man who said his legs hurt, but didn't have any legs. Mel had her colouring book that helped her relax. Others were bent over tables in the safe injection area, under the fluorescent lights. Buster, the rescue dog who technically belonged to Mel but really belonged to everyone, was making his wagging rounds.

The shelter had sprung up four winters prior, intended to be temporary, in a vacant warehouse-turned-failed-nightclub, not the first business along Leon to close its doors. The Mission Shelter was down the street; anyone could stay there as long as there was room. Hearthstone was different. You could reserve a bed, and it was yours. When it first opened there were seventy-five mats on the floor. All were occupied that first week. Since then, the mats had been replaced by permanent beds. There was a waiting list for people wanting a spot.

"Have you heard from her at all?"

"Nope." There was an edge to Cerise's voice, but she gave Kayla a sideways hug, their usual greeting. They had their differences—Cerise had opinions about everything, and just because Kayla was more of a watcher and a listener didn't mean she didn't have her own—but they also shared so much: the work, the hustle, the cold nights, the clients whose needs were often for more than sex.

Those who worked the streets knew how to communicate with their eyes. They trusted each other to memorize licence plates, speak without speaking. And most nights they got ready together, putting on makeup along with the identity they would assume for the night. They shared all that, and they shared the stories and the laughter too, because working these streets, you needed to share that to keep going.

And now it was another night. Rinse and repeat. She had spent the day as she usually did. She'd had breakfast at the Mission's soup kitchen. Then, as soon as it opened, she went to the library. There, despite the sign in the washroom—*You Must Be Awake, Sober & Respectful to Use This Space—No Illegal Drugs, Substances, or Alcohol Use or Possession—No Grooming, Bathing, Shaving, Etc.*—she washed up in the washroom. Then she'd headed to the second-storey study carrels, where she caught some warmth and rest. She spent the day there, listening to audiobooks and sharing pastries snuck in by Habiba, the hijab-wearing physics student who was also there so much. Then, when the library closed, she'd gone to Hearthstone to meet up with Cerise and Little Zoe, get ready for the night.

"It was chili today," Cerise said, pointing with her chin towards a folding table at the back of the room. There sat a crockpot and coffee maker, paper plates and cups, hopeful salad.

The chili was hot and good. As she ate, Kayla stared at the walls adorned with taped-up art—some spray-painted, tattoo designs of skeletons and swords, one startlingly realistic portrait of an old man. Printed out signs read: *Take only what you are going to eat. Please keep our washrooms clean! No smoking. No needles in your bunk.* Another sign listed the hours of a walk-in clinic. A chalkboard was scrawled with messages: *Kelsey—Josh got into rehab, will text you when can. Steve—text your case worker. Eli—call your mother.* At the margins of the chalkboard were graffiti tags in chalk, a rose with delicate shading, a shaky happy face. There was another memorial poster up, one for a tattooed man in a baseball cap holding a baby. Kayla realized it was the face of someone familiar, the face fuller and more smiling than the one she had known.

"Was last night quiet for you, too?" Cerise asked, brushing her cherry-coloured hair. They usually watched each other get into cars, so knew how busy a night it was, but it was easy to lose track if you were both on dates at the same time.

"It was okay." It had been much better than okay, but she didn't want her friend to feel any envy. Kayla's fingers traced the smoothness of Little Zoe's duvet. "Where do you think she is?"

"Hopefully off making good money." Cerise smirked. She got jealous when she thought Little Zoe was making more than the rest of them. Cerise had watched the newer, younger girls come and go, watched them take more clients and charge higher. She always vied for as much as she could make, of course—she wasn't like those who charged just enough for a fix (unless things were bad enough)—but she also knew younger girls like Little Zoe or Kayla would always be chosen first. Cerise had seen it all before in Vancouver, back when she had been the one chosen first. She had started out high track. She'd earned enough not just for sweet clothes but for a nice apartment, and all the things she never would have been able to afford had she kept slinging burgers, her manager brushing too close against her and taking liberties with his hands.

And she didn't think of her business as selling herself. She rented parts of her body out, but not her head and not her heart.

That was where Little Zoe failed—or succeeded, depending on how you saw it. Like Kayla and Cerise, with her words or with her body, she could tell a story to clients and have them believe. But unlike them, she had been known to give a bit more.

Take Thursday Man, for instance. When he first started coming around, he would go for any of the girls. He would circle the block, slowing, until he worked up the courage to pull over. Once on a date, he was jumpy, polite. The women wondered if part of the reason he wanted to spend time with them was to practice his English.

"His co-workers make fun of him," Little Zoe had explained after their first date. "He likes someone who won't laugh." Then she clarified. "He likes to laugh. Just not about that."

No one but Little Zoe had heard him laugh.

After his first date with Little Zoe, he never chose one of the other women again. He came not just Thursdays, but Fridays too. Then also Mondays at lunch. Little Zoe acquired a new dress, a new phone. She also acquired a protectiveness about him. Wouldn't let the others say a word.

And it wasn't just him. Little Zoe knew who needed to feel big and who needed to feel small, who wanted their rough edges to be smoothed and who needed to be roughened. She could tell who needed to feel powerful and respected, and who needed to lick the bottoms of her stilettos. She would make up whatever stories they needed to hear, listen to whatever stories they needed to tell.

And Little Zoe's kindness wasn't reserved just for the johns. She would lend money when you needed it. And she would listen when you needed it too. With Derek, days when he wore his fishing hat because his ideas were flowing fast, she shared her time, encouraged him to go on. For Mama B or Gloria, whose bodies reflected their years, she was there to help set up their tents or run an errand. She would help Lily with the bandages on her bad arm. And when Alexa's bag was stolen, Little Zoe gave her makeup, including her best foundation, because Alexa needed it more, to hide the stubble that no longer belonged to who she was.

In the same way Nelson could repair an old Walkman or MacGyver a broken cart, Little Zoe knew how to fix what needed fixing, heal what had been hurt. She was able to see the good and special in someone when they could not see it in themselves. She knew how to divine something hidden, buried, even if yet unformed. She knew how to ask the questions that mattered.

Kayla had her first real conversation with Little Zoe when the autumn leaves had just started to turn, not long after Kayla had arrived in town. Little Zoe had brought her to sit on the sand by the lake. They were far enough from the playground that you couldn't hear the children. Kayla didn't yet know that the sounds of their laughter made her friend sad.

Little Zoe was in her bikini and wearing the unicorn necklace that one of the street outreach workers had given her. Songs were floating from the boats across the water, seagulls flew above. The sun was shining on her face.

"So what do you love most, Kayla?" Little Zoe had asked.

Kayla was silent. What she loved most?

"What I loved..." She stopped. Saying it out loud would only bring the pain of its absence.

"It matters," Little Zoe said, looking at Kayla harder than she expected. "As a kid, I didn't get a chance to love for long, usually, so I choose to love a lot wherever I am. Right in that moment."

Kayla looked down. Her love had been deep too, once. She thought of the barn, of the horses, of the footsteps she had heard one morning.

"No matter what you've been through, you still have that," Little Zoe continued. "Ask yourself what you love, and love it. Love it anyway."

And as Kayla came to know, as autumn leaves fell, as the weather paled into winter, Little Zoe's love was as big as she was little. From the morning's first hint of light to the music drifting through the alleys—how the songs overlapped, separate, but together making something new—in all she saw, in all she did, she loved well and she loved hard.

And for all the people and things she loved, Little Zoe also loved heroin. She had loved and hated it, and loved it more, ever since she was a girl.

"My foster sister—my sister—was the one who first shot me up," she told Kayla that afternoon.

They had lain in the sand, far enough from families soaking up the last days of warmth, pedicured teenagers in bikinis. They had watched mothers open up picnic coolers of food, offering it to their kids: watermelon slices and peanut butter sandwiches, Freezies half melted in the heat.

"She said it would make it easier. Erase the pain, you know? She wasn't a bad person. She shot me up to protect me. She did what worked for her."

The boats on the water, a toddler in water wings, the sunlight on Little Zoe's shoulders.

"I'd been at that place a while. My foster father—he—the heroin was to make it easier for me, you know? He would come into our room. He'd come over to us even at the kitchen table. My foster mother would already be passed out in the other room. Or he'd do it when she was in the same room, if she was gone enough."

Kayla remembered the lingering warmth of the sand, light playing on the lake, how Little Zoe's rawness was a gift. Something sacred that she was giving Kayla.

"That was the summer when I started to get boobs, you see. When my sister started me on it." She paused. "He waited until I grew boobs. He wasn't all bad. He wouldn't have abused a little kid."

*

"Maybe we'll see her once we're out there," Cerise said, tucking her makeup bag under her bed, the shelter busy all around. Kayla could tell she needed to get to work to pay for her fix. They walked past the rows and rows of beds, past Kori who was sorting her resale items, past the woman who would bring folks chili if they weren't up for getting it themselves, past the new shelter worker who still believed anything was possible, past the girl who always sang the same song, and into the thickness of the night.

Saturday, 7:30 p.m.

There were candles. That was the first thing Kayla saw when she and Cerise stepped out onto Leon Avenue.

Beyond the usual smattering of women standing around smoking, men in pulled-up hoodies sitting on bikes, and Marta with her brimming cart, a cluster of people were gathered around. In the middle of them was a cake. Someone was singing, 'Happy Birthday'.

Naomi stood near the curb. Mama B held the cake in front of her, both their faces lit. Around them were folks from Hearthstone and the street.

Mama B was singing away, grinning with no teeth. Some people who walked by her as she panhandled could have taken her for a hard woman if they didn't stop to talk—sitting on that sidewalk, her mouth a straight line, jaw jutting—but there was a smile there if anyone looked long enough to see. Mama B had her bad places but had spent long enough in them that she didn't dwell there now.

Teflon pulled out her knife. Her hands glinted with the many rings she wore as brass knuckles. Rings were not illegal. She went to cut the cake, but Naomi reached out and stopped her.

"Hold on. I want pictures." Naomi reached into the pocket of her coat, which was sewn with patches from punk bands and anarchy slogans. Hanging below her coat was the too-big hoodie she wore every day, the one that said, *All Cats Are Beautiful.* Kayla liked what it said on the back: *an injury to one is an injury to all.*

Naomi pulled out her phone from one of the big pockets. She used them to liberate food from store shelves and casually dipping into the bulk food aisles at the grocery (only big-box stores, never Ma and Pa places). There, she would grab fistfuls of nuts and seeds and candies. Once, she had returned from Superstore with pockets full of olives from the deli bar.

"Such a beautiful cake," she murmured, taking pictures and having fun with different angles.

Marcel, with whom she shared her love and her tent—a home that didn't look like a home to most—stood beside her. He was a fruit picker from Quebec. In summers, he worked the fields and orchards. He would bring buckets of discarded fruit for folks on Leon, along with the best that he secretly saved from the fields. When Kayla had first arrived in town, she had been surprised to see so many peach pits on the sidewalk. Like everything and everyone else, they got swept up by the city each morning, but Marcel would always bring more.

"Let me get some pictures with you too," Lily said, taking the phone. She took one of Naomi and the cake, one of Marcel, and then one of them together, with Buster in the picture too. Then Lily panned to Alexa, smiling in her extra long eyelashes and the necklace she had procured for herself to honour the day that she had stopped answering to Alex. Underneath her faux fur coat was the dress she'd been so proud to sew (back when she had access to a sewing machine): a sparkly magenta creation she'd designed to accommodate her shoulders and tall frame. She dreamed of starting her own fashion line, sparkly dresses that celebrated all forms.

"Get more of the cake," Mama B instructed. "I got that lettering done special."

And she had. She hadn't stolen the cake, not because stealing a cake was out of her repertoire, but because she wanted it iced: *Happy Birthday Naomi*, in turquoise, Naomi's favourite colour. Mama B bought it at Safeway, she would explain again and again as people came and went. (And she wouldn't have stolen from Safeway anyway. Safeway didn't make a fuss if you wanted to use the washroom, and they were generous with their day-olds and produce past its prime. It would have been rude to steal from them.) No, Mama B had counted out the change that she got from panhandling, letting all those in line see that she was a paying customer just like them. It was a beautiful chocolate cake, rosettes and all. And with turquoise.

Teflon began to cut the cake. Her hands were steady, just as they usually were, whether she had someone in a chokehold or was stabbing someone in the thigh with Naloxone after an overdose, bringing them back to life. She was known for being good at both.

"I owe ya a song," Dan-o said. "I'll play for you when the piano is out in the park for the summer. I'll play you a great song."

Kayla watched, taking it all in, feeling warm despite the cold.

From behind a couple of the others, someone stepped forward, hood pulled up, grey beard hanging below, pant hems dragging—Old Nelson. He didn't say anything, just held out a ceramic vase. A profound crack snaked across the top; it had clearly once been in pieces, but he had found a way to put it back together again.

"For your flowers." His voice was as rough as his hands.

Naomi smiled. She had spent the summer giving out flowers on Leon Avenue, gifting people she knew and people she didn't know yet with roses from the City's plantings. She believed more in sharing joy than in private property.

"I love it."

It was a surprise to see Nelson here. He kept to himself except when he ran out of both drink and money. He was the last person anyone would expect at a party. But Kayla had seen, one night while curled in her sleeping bag on the street, that Naomi had been there to comfort him when he had one of his dreams that woke him up screaming. She never mentioned it to him in the morning, never mentioned it to anyone at all.

A mickey was being passed around. Buster was by now served his own slice of cake.

"Don't feed chocolate to dogs," Lily was saying.

"Maybe it's not real chocolate," someone else said. "It's fine."

"It's fucking real chocolate."

"You want another piece of cake?" Gloria asked her new street daughter, Sally. The girl had come from a reserve up north not long ago. Although she was of a different Nation, Gloria saw Sally as her own. Her biological children had been taken, lost to the child welfare system she described as residential schools in different clothes. She could have grandchildren out there even. But she kept her street daughters close. She taught them a few words of her first language, nsyilxcən, and how to do beadwork—their own designs as well as the old ways—along with how to survive on the streets.

"Yeah. Yeah, I'd like another slice," Sally said. "And one of those rosettes."

As people dug into their cake, Kayla asked what she couldn't get out of her mind. "Anyone seen Little Zoe?"

Shaking heads all around.

"She's missing out," Lily sighed. "This cake is really good."

But it wasn't the first time Little Zoe just disappeared, Kayla reassured herself. She always came back with a reason, with tales.

"And where's Ketchum, anyway?"

"Don't know, but that motherfucker returned my bike again," Teflon said. She had taken a bike from someone's porch, one with children's streamers on the handlebars, and Ketchum had returned it. Some things were not for stealing, according to his code. She had stolen it back. And now, apparently, so had he again.

"He said he was going back to the woods," Naomi told her. "Needed some time to himself."

"That and the cops were looking for him," Teflon added.

Ketchum was a dear friend who been there for Kayla time and time again, but he spent most nights in the woods near the encampment of unhoused folks behind Enterprise Road: Tent City. He hunkered down in a shack made of wooden pallets he had built himself.

"These rosettes are so good," Sally was saying. "Haven't had these since I was a little girl."

Time passed. Stories got told, sometimes told again. No one hurried. Here was the only place they had to be.

Lily held up Naomi's phone. "Shit. It's out of battery."

She'd gone from taking pictures of the party to snapping selfies, plus some of her with Sally. Lily had plans to put an escort ad online and earn some better money. The pics of her with Sally would be perfect for advertising duos. Sally still looked so fresh and new. And their ethnic combo had to be someone's flavour.

Naomi's face fell just a bit.

It was the disappointment in Naomi's eyes that made Kayla take out her own phone. She knew, from the photographs she kept tucked away in her backpack—one of her dad, one of her grandma, one of a horse she'd once loved, Buddy—how important having something from these moments could be.

The first picture Kayla took was of Naomi and Marcel, arms around each other, the patch on Naomi's coat reading *UNITE*. Marcel had on a hoodie with a drawing of a guitar, a paintbrush, and a pen, and *These Weapons Slay Injustice.* He also had a sword tattooed on his neck. He'd once explained to Kayla that he got it to commemorate a bar fight in which he'd knifed someone, in a time of life he'd long left behind.

Kayla got a picture of Mel with Sally after that. Mel was in a Big White Ski Resort coat. Sally was dressed for work, wearing the scuffed high heels she had learned to walk in. She was new to going with men for money and had never been attracted to men at all, but the work had nothing to do with attraction. Mel understood her girlfriend had to work. Work was work. Straight for pay was no exception. And Mel would look out for Sally, Kayla knew. The picture was completed by a stellar photobomb from Buster, with icing on his nose.

Kayla got a picture of Derek too. He was having a good night, happy to be around people who didn't just keep walking when he tried to speak, who didn't hate him after the bad nights, because everyone had bad nights in their own ways.

Even Teflon was smiling that night.

Kayla wanted to get a picture of Nelson, too—surely no one had taken one of him in a while. She wondered if the flash would bother him the way fireworks did, but he was already gone.

"Okay, everyone, gather 'round," Mama B was saying. "Let's get a picture of us all together."

Try as they did, it was hard to gather everyone. Some didn't know where to stand; some wanted to be front and centre; some were uncertain if they should be in the picture at all. After a little shuffling and last-minute grabs and ducks and arms around each other, it was far from perfect, but everyone came together, such as they were.

"Cerise," Kayla called over. She realized she didn't have a single picture of her closest friends. Not even one of Little Zoe. "Let me get a good one of you before we go."

Kayla tried. What she captured was not exactly what she was aiming for, but was very much Cerise. She wasn't quite smiling, but neither did she have the steeled, unflinching look she knew how to give. She was just looking sideways, as if searching for the next thing, for something just out of view.

All that was missing from that night was a certain laugh, a certain way of putting arms around another. Little Zoe had a stronger grip than you would expect from someone so small. She had a way of giving a hug that was not possessiveness—more a sharing of strength. And her laugh. She would toss her head back and smile wide, that one tooth missing, laughing into the sky, eyes as bright as stars.

Saturday, 9:00 p.m.

"Stall them!"

Kayla heard him before she saw him: a man hurtling past on his bike, hoodie up, silhouetted by the streetlights. After the party had ended—the cops cruised by and everyone knew it was time to disperse—she'd been walking to the corner where she worked.

Just before he disappeared into the darkness of an alley, she realized the man on the bike was Ketchum. She also saw the police cruiser coming up Leon Avenue, lights flashing. Not knowing exactly what was up, but figuring Ketchum needed her help, she grabbed her stomach, crumpled over, and staggered into the street in front of the cop car, a look of agony on her face.

Brakes screeching, the cop car stopped just in front of her.

"Can we help you?" The officer had the window down. He looked pissed, but no one wanted someone dead on their shift if they could help it.

"Oh god, it hurts so bad," Kayla groaned, clutching her stomach. She glanced down the alley where Ketchum had darted. No sign of him. "But I think it's going away. Sorry to bother you."

"Should we call an ambulance?"

Kayla stood slowly, but stayed put. "Just give me a sec. I'll be okay. Sorry."

Time bought, job done, she staggered back to the curb.

She watched the cops pull away and snake down the alley, from which Ketchum would be long gone.

Ketchum was not one to be caught. Not on the streets and not in his former life—no one in the casinos could catch him at blackjack or poker. He had originally gone by Blackjack Ketchum because he'd been a shark who could pay for his family's trips to Vegas with his winnings. But that was a long time ago.

Kayla had first met him one night after a date had put her in no mood to work. It was a night when her memories scratched hard, when she thought she should quit street work for good, and do anything, anything different.

"You need help?" he had asked, keeping a few feet away, the way you approach a hurt animal who might scratch.

"I'm fine," she had insisted. "I'm fine."

"Want me to go after that fucker?" The car was stopped at an intersection not far away.

"I just want the night to be over." She had needed a moment to gather herself.

"You alright though?"

When he turned to her, she was struck by his eyes. There were many layers there, she could see, and kindness was one.

"You want company?" Then he quickly shook his head. "Not that kind."

Kayla wanted to be alone but not alone all at once. She sat down on the curb, the streetlight on her back. He sat too, but far enough away.

"You ever want me to do anything to anyone for you, I would," he said at last, like violence was a language he spoke, was what he knew how to offer.

"Thanks." Then she realized the bite in her tone, abrasive and difficult as her night had been. "No need to go after anyone though." She looked at him then and saw what he had been willing to give. "But really, thank you." She'd seen enough of violence, never wanted more of it.

"Everyone needs someone on their side sometimes. You ever need anything, I mean it for real. You...you remind me a bit of my old girlfriend."

Here it comes, Kayla had thought, leaning further away.

"Lost her to an OD last summer, when the drugs were really strong. The fuckin' elephant tranquilizer. Loved that woman. She didn't have all her pieces together, but she knew how to pick up mine. Or try. And she tried..."

Kayla wasn't sure what to say.

"I know she thinks of me. She sends me messages. If a streetlight turns on, or one of the ducks on Leon stops and stares at me, I know she's trying to communicate. And sometimes certain words jump out in graffiti and I feel...well, to say it out loud, it sounds crazy. And I know she can't be here. But in a way, she always will be..."

They sat in silence again.

"I used to build houses," he said out of nowhere, then, holding out his hands: "There's something about turning those raw materials into something with your own hands, you know?"

Under the glow of the streetlight, his hands reminded Kayla of the strong, calloused hands she'd had working on the farm.

"I learned how to build from my foster father. He took me in because he wanted someone to work for free. But I liked the work. Eventually got old enough to leave and find a paying gig. But construction is a young person's job. Got hurt. Fucked my back. So now I do what I can. But some days I still walk around those subdivisions, see families there, trees growing, the things I built come to life."

He looked over towards where a few people had gathered in the doorway of the closed pub, the glow of a lighter between them. The glint of a spoon.

"Worked on the killing floor of a slaughterhouse too," he said after a pause. "I'm not afraid of any work, but that's the worst work there is."

He took a cigarette from his pocket, lit it, took a slow drag.

"No one wants that job, so you work with lots of other guys who don't have a choice either. Not many spoke English. But we all learned the same language: how to kill."

He wiped his hands on his jeans.

"The animals in there...I'll never forget those eyes. The look in their eyes before I killed them. It was a wild look, but also not wild at all. Hardly different than a human. It was like looking at yourself at your most scared."

Kayla looked at him then, but he was just looking down at his hands.

"At the end of the day, you have your conscience, and that... well, you can't rinse that clean. Some nights, I would just wash my hands, just keep washing them. But your mind—that's harder to wash."

He wiped his hands on his jeans again.

"Sometimes they wouldn't die right away. They'd look at you as life drained out of them. And...and...some of the guys, the things they'd do to them when they are still alive..."

Kayla wondered if she should touch his hand. But she just looked at him.

"When you have no choice, you can do horrible things. But I never wanted to do horrible things."

She reached out to him with comfort in her arms, offering what she could offer.

"But you, you don't seem like you've had blood on your hands," he said to her.

"Actually," she said, looking out into the darkness, "I have."

It was the closest she had come to saying any of it out loud.

Saturday, 10:00 p.m.

"You free tonight." The man in the Lamborghini had not phrased it as a question.

Free: Kayla thought of how much that word could mean, in so many ways. She was standing with Cerise when the Lambo pulled up. The man driving wore sunglasses despite the dark. The motor purred. He motioned to Kayla.

"Lucky bitch," Cerise mouthed. "Go girl."

From how the man spoke, with the window lowered just a bit, he was not new at this. He knew what to say, what not to say. When the price was settled, Kayla heard the doors unlock. She slid into the car and tucked her backpack at her feet. He looked at it, then at her. Cerise and Little Zoe would have let Kayla store her pack at Hearthstone if she wanted, but it held all she owned, and it was anything but a deterrent for business. Some johns seemed to like the idea that she had nowhere else to go.

"I know a place," she told the man, with a surety of voice she hadn't known months ago, though this was far from how she had pictured herself making a living back when she'd been working on the farm.

Kayla started going with johns once her money was gone, after hitching across the country in a horse trailer back in August and scraping by until she couldn't. Given what she'd left behind, there was no way she was going to use her ID to get an official job—she hadn't even told anyone out here her full name.

On these streets she could work for herself. It wasn't a town where you needed a pimp. She could've worked the indoor track, but the massage parlour downtown took most of your money, and you had no control over your hours, your clients, or what actually happened. They probably required ID, too. On the street the terms weren't always pretty, but they were yours.

But despite earning good money sometimes, it wasn't enough for first and last month's rent. And housing was at a premium in this city. More than that, everyone said she would have to show her ID to secure an apartment. So for now she concentrated on getting by.

Even if you didn't have an addiction—Kayla did not—money was hard to keep on the street. She'd had her money stolen out here three times. She had to keep what she earned on her. It was impossible to get a bank account without an address. When she was new out here, her earnings had disappeared from her pack at a shelter once. The second time she was held up with bear spray by a guy on the street. The third time, a john had robbed her.

"So yeah," she told him, infusing confidence in her voice. "I know a good place to go."

"I know a spot," the Lambo man said.

"There's a perfect spot just down the street. Quiet and dark."

"I said I have a spot. And I've already paid."

The Lamborghini wound out of downtown, past the hospital, past the banks and beachside hotels and fast-food drive-thrus. They sailed past schools with paper hearts in the windows, nice big houses, white-picket fences, estates surrounded by tall metal spikes. They zipped past manicured gardens, SUVs and sports cars in circular driveways, boats. It was a world away. The only constant was the long lake beside them.

They continued until only trees began to flank the road. They were going further than Kayla wanted.

She thought about not having seen Little Zoe since the night before. But Little Zoe always said there was a balance between staying chilled and having a healthy fear, being aware of your surroundings and situation. *Always listen to yourself. Always know when it's time to go.* But how could you know for sure before it was too late?

The houses lining the road grew sparse. Sumacs and weeping willows flashed in the headlights.

The man kept his eyes straight ahead. "You from here?"

"No." Though she made up truths to suit the situation, this was actually the case. She was from Guelph, a midsized city in Ontario, where she'd lived until that one night in August when she'd brought a backpack of a few hastily gathered belongings, a wool horse blanket, and a desire to get away in that moment. "You?" She hadn't taken him as the chatty type. But she wanted to keep everything normal.

"No." Streetlights illuminated him and then cast him back into darkness, again and again.

She couldn't help but think of Little Zoe, but everything was probably fine. She often convinced johns to keep her longer than they planned, to spend a whole night in a hotel, enjoy a hot shower and a nice bed. Once she'd been gone three days for a houseboat party on Shuswap Lake. And she had disappeared for a week when some guys who worked the oil sands camps in Fort McMurray brought her up north to party. They worked fourteen days on, seven days off, and had no shortage of money or lonely desire. Their week off was her week on.

Sure, she had a phone, but there were many reasons why she might have been parted from it. Lots of reasonable explanations.

Where are you? Message me, Kayla texted her, again, as the Lamborghini man continued to drive. More dark blurs of sumacs and pines flanked the roadside. Eventually, gravel crunched as the car pulled into the drive of a secluded beach.

SWIM AT OWN RISK, the sign read. NO LIFEGUARD ON DUTY. THIS IS A DESIGNATED DOG BEACH. But there were no dogs, and no people, at this hour.

He turned off the ignition.

Her pocketed hands were worrying the bills he had given her, crisp. By now she had learned to make them pay her first.

Staring straight ahead, he grabbed her around the wrist. Then he reached towards the glove compartment.

She could barely breathe.

He reached behind a neat stack of papers, an owner's manual, and an organizer book. He grabbed something in his hands, closed the latch of the glove compartment. Then he handed her a condom and a hair elastic.

"I like to see."

*

As soon as she finished with the Lamborghini man, Kayla grabbed her backpack and stepped from the car. He'd said he'd take her back to the city, but something about the quiet solitude out here made her want to stay, and she didn't want to risk being with him further. She stood in the cold and watched the taillights grow smaller.

The beach was dark save for the moon and the few streetlights that bordered the distant road. The lake was smooth. High up in the black mountains across the water, valleys of snow were light against the darkness.

Kayla unzipped her boots. Even though the air was cold on her feet, taking them off felt good. She walked over the stones to the water's edge, bent, cupped the water with her hands, brought it to her mouth, and rinsed.

Quickly as it came, she banished the thought of another night last summer when she had rinsed her mouth like this.

But not like this. Not like this at all.

The water on that night had been from a culvert just past the horse farm, brackish and horrible, mixing with blood.

Shards of memory cut deep and sudden.

Trying to think of something else, she recalled how much Little Zoe loved to float in this very lake, loving the water, laughing like the child she had never fully been able to be. Some nights, downtown, she would strip down and wade into the darkness of the lake. Little Zoe said floating there let her feel the freest she could feel. *Free. I never feel more free.*

Sunday, 5:00 a.m.

Kayla walked in the company of the moon. Her bad leg hurt. She was barely awake from the few hours of sleep she had caught at the beach before the cold coming off the lake woke her.

She checked her phone. Still nothing from Little Zoe.

With the night's earnings tucked in her bra, she walked toward the orange glow of the city. The road back from the dog beach followed the lake, lights from the west side glimmering from across the water. Dark plumes of forest flanked the other side of the road, along with rows and rows of orchards, branches like gnarled fingers reaching towards the inky sky.

When a car came by, slowing, she thought of hitching, but she'd had enough adrenaline for one night. And the quiet was so peaceful. The first seam of light was paling at the horizon.

The houses became more frequent as she walked on, a few squares of light appearing in them as morning approached. She passed a horse farm, paddock fences pale in the scant light. No horses were yet turned out in those fields, but there was a light in the barn.

She just stood there, breathing in to see if she could catch any scent, any trace of what she missed so much. She thought of who must be in that barn this early, feeding the horses before the day began. Someone like she had once been.

Three years ago, at sixteen, as soon as it was legal, she had moved into a drafty bachelor apartment in the local horse barn. She got the place and a little extra cash in exchange for working as a stable hand. Her days had started while it was still dark—measuring out the horses' feed, doling out hay, turning them out in their paddocks, mucking the stalls—days that didn't end until it was dark again.

She had lived in fear of the stable owner, Patricia, a sinewy woman with a temper and a belief that things were to be done exactly one way. Her husband, John, was a quiet man who drove the tractor or watched the riding lessons. Then there was Carl, who took care of the horses on weekdays, and Demi Ray, the horse trainer who was the first to show Kayla that you didn't need size to have a presence.

Kayla had been hanging around that barn since she was twelve, mucking stalls on weekends in exchange for one riding lesson per week. The barn was within biking distance of Kayla's place, and she had gone there as often as she could. She would watch the horses in the fields, brush them, do whatever it took to be around them; she would scoop manure, sweep the aisles of the barn, stack hay bales, scrub feed buckets, clean brushes, oil saddles and bridles, do whatever was put before her, until her hands were raw. All for the one hour a week when she could ride.

She always chose Buddy, a plain bay gelding the stable owner had picked up at a meat auction. Riding, Kayla felt a connection, strength, and freedom she hadn't known possible. In harmony with another being, she felt a wordless closeness she hadn't known existed. She could leave her thoughts and worries behind like the dust that settled in the wake of those hooves. Riding, nothing could catch her or hold her down.

When Carl left a gate open and let the horses run loose across the road, it wasn't his first offence on the farm, but it was his last. Patricia fired him, knowing full well Kayla was old enough to drop out of school and that she wouldn't say no.

The apartment next to the feed room was just a one-windowed room barely big enough to fit a bed, and uninsulated besides, but at least it wasn't the home of her childhood—it was hers. The small amount of cash she'd get paid could buy enough to eat.

She remembered the day that she stood at its doorway. Carl, who'd lived there, had left in a hurry, and the bed was still covered with twisted, hay-flecked blankets. Food-encrusted dishes, an empty whiskey bottle, a mug with dead flies at the bottom, and feed catalogue sat on a plastic patio chair beside the bed along with a nasty-smelling bucket. The floor had been swept far less frequently than the aisles of the barn.

"Fucking bastard had a hot plate," Patricia noted, standing beside her and surveying the place, no doubt thinking of fire. Kayla hadn't yet thought of how she was going to cook, and she didn't care. She could live on instant oatmeal and ramen noodles.

She had brought only a backpack of belongings from the apartment that she shared with her mother and her mother's latest boyfriend. She put Carl's bottles in the garbage, pulled the blanket over the bed, and sat there. Breathed.

There had been no fanfare when she left: her mother treated the live-in accommodations as part of Kayla's job, as a sign of growing up, not as the big moment of leaving home. Work was something inevitable, to be endured. Her mother was a server at a 24-hour diner. Back from her shift, she would talk to herself, hashing out the days with an anger so deep it must have had little to do with the restaurant. She always ended the day—whatever time it was—by soaking her feet in the company of a glass of Jack Daniels. And never just one.

Her mother's drinking only really started when Kayla was four, after Kayla's father was killed. A car accident. Kayla had fond, fuzzy memories of those early days, but her dad was little more than a shadowy wish. She remembered the smell of motor oil on him from his work with cars, his body warm and big and loving as he hugged her. She remembered how he could raise a car up on a hoist, above their heads, like magic, how he could jump so high at the basketball court, and how he would lift her up, above his shoulders, so she could put the ball into the net just like he did, how strong and kind and right his arms were around her as they cuddled in front of the TV. She didn't remember what shows they watched—just those hugging arms and the warm lap where all felt right with the world. Until one day he never came back.

And then her mother cried a lot and slept a lot. And became friends with Jack Daniels.

Childhood had been a stretch of watching early morning cartoons with the volume turned down low, chewing her cereal quietly so as not to wake the unpredictable woman who slept on the other side of the wall. Until she met friends who had babysitters, she thought nothing of being left alone evenings while her mother worked, playing with her dolls but keeping their voices silent except for in her head. She had trained herself to stay quiet and undetectable. She took care to avoid starting the flares of anger that ignited within her mother, potential flares that Kayla taught herself to prevent before they burst into full flame.

And then there was her mother's boyfriend. Not any of the ones who lived there later. Those ones Kayla could take or leave: the sweet ones and the ignoring ones, the loud ones and the quiet ones, the ones who bought her gifts or attempted to tell jokes or tried to help her with her homework, the ones who came and went and sometimes made her mother sad and sometimes made her mother happy and sometimes paid the rent. Not them.

But the one who had been there before, that first one. The one she called—That One.

Even after he was gone he wasn't gone.

When the barn owner left the apartment that first day and Kayla had the place to herself, she had just stood in that small room, marvelling that it was all hers now. Even the feed bucket by the side of the bed, with its thin layer of liquid reeking of vomit and liquor, did nothing to deter her. Like all else, it could become clean.

That first night, tightening the musty blankets around herself, surrounded by the smells of horses and hay and the mulchy deepness of the barn, she could hear the animals in their stalls, their sighs and breaths and nighttime noises that only she could hear, and, perhaps for the first time, she felt that she was home.

Sunday, 7:00 a.m.

Home, now, was Leon Avenue.

Light had stirred itself into the sky by the time Kayla reached downtown. Before businesses opened, before cars or people heading to work were on the street, the city felt like hers.

She came by Marta, ensconced in blankets and not looking up from her knitting. With yarn that a church group gave her, she knitted hats and mittens for herself and other folks out here. And she knitted the blanket she had named Always. That blanket was always growing because she stitched a new zigzag row of colour to commemorate each person lost. Fentanyl was rampant in the drug supply. These days Marta needed a steady supply of yarn.

Further down the street was Gloria, sitting outside her tent, which she had set up outside the Ki-Low-Na Friendship Society, a community base for Indigenous folks. The society wasn't open yet, but Gloria was ready to be there for anyone who needed it. On this morning, it was just her and Sally. The girl, with her raven hair streaked with fuchsia (Cerise had shared her hair dye), had a sleeping bag around her shoulders. She and Gloria sat around a metal kettle placed over the flame of a camp burner.

"Morning," Gloria said, holding up a chipped mug. "Want some tea?"

Gloria collected herbs and medicines that grew wild by Knox Mountain, north of downtown. From teas to poultices to ointments, she had cures for many things. Except addiction, to which she had already lost her other street daughter before Sally came.

"I'm good, thanks," Kayla answered. Though she was tempted by the promise of its warmth, she could see the empty water bottle beside Gloria's foot. There would be just enough water in that kettle for Gloria and Sally, and to get more they would have to trek over to the public washrooms in City Park. So Kayla wouldn't impose.

"How are you?" Kayla's voice was hoarse from not talking since the night before.

"I'm alive, so it's a good day," Gloria chuckled. She pulled out a handful of the sugar packets that she grabbed every time she bought her one coffee a day at Timmies. She said she liked her tea sweet, because life hadn't been. "You, you look tired. Get some rest."

Then Kayla saw Mama B, outside her own tent further down the street.

"You weren't in your usual spot last night," Mama B called over. Mama B checked in on folks. Coming from Vancouver's downtown east side, those stretches of East Hastings where so many street folks lived, she had been used to constant comings and goings.

"You just getting in?" Mama B looked at Kayla in her boots and mini kilt, the leggings she had put on for warmth. Then Mama B coughed that cough that was always with her, getting worse.

"Just walked back from the dog beach on Lakeshore Road."

Mama B made a little whistling noise. "That's plenty far. And those boots..."

"It was far." But Kayla had other things on her mind. "You see Little Zoe last night?"

"Can't say I did."

"I didn't see her yesterday either. And Cerise said she never got back the night before."

"Well, we all know she's a busy girl." Mama B had been around long enough to know people came and went, came and went, doing what they had to do, going where their journeys took them. But there a flicker of worry in her eyes. Like the rest, Mama B also knew the drug supply was unpredictable these days, that overdoses were on the rise. The idea of Little Zoe, alone in a hotel room, celebrating good earnings, taking in too much, had already crossed Kayla's mind.

So had the spectre of a bad date of the very worst kind.

The remains of a woman who worked the streets had been found on a farm in the northern part of the Okanagan Valley a few years back. Police searched the property after hearing rumours from the street about a man who had already been convicted of assaulting sex workers. That woman's death was still under investigation, but everyone on the street had their suspicions. Four more women in the Okanagan had gone missing. All were

Indigenous, as were too many of the women who had gone missing further north of the valley. And those on the street had all heard about a man with a boat who took girls out to party on the lake. Apparently one of the girls, an escort, never came back from a boat ride. Kayla hadn't known her. That woman had her own back-page ad, but never worked the street. There was an ongoing investigation into her, too.

"I'm sure Little Zoe will turn up soon," Mama B said, offering a consoling smile. "She usually good on text?"

"Usually." Except when she wasn't. Except when she lost her phone or let the battery go dead. Except when she was busy. But two nights with no message?

Mama B reached out and gave Kayla's hand a squeeze. "I'll keep my ears and eyes open. Now you got anything warmer to change into?"

"I'm okay. Thanks. And thanks for keeping an eye out."

"Of course. It's what I do."

Kayla continued up Leon. Naomi and Marcel were packing up their tent, as they always did first thing. They weren't ones for involvement with bylaw or the cops, not since Naomi had been arrested for not moving during a street sweep before the start of tourist season. She'd been charged for obstructing justice and disturbing the peace.

"You want a Pop-Tart?" Naomi held out a box.

Naomi looked out for the working girls. She saw what they did as different from wage labour in the capitalist machine, of which she refused to be a part.

"And here," Marcel said, handing Kayla a protein bar. The outreach volunteers gave those out. Marcel handed them back to folks who needed them more. He was a provider in his own way.

"Thanks so much," Kayla said, realizing her hunger now that she could. Sometimes, walking, she could get past feeling it. "Did either of you see Little Zoe last night? Or yesterday?"

"Don't think so," Marcel said.

Naomi paused. "Me neither. But she's on her own clock."

True.

"You hear about Teflon?" Naomi continued, as if nothing was wrong. "She's got new charges. They're looking for her. So keep an eye out for her too."

Teflon called herself Teflon because nothing stuck to her—not people, not her past, and, usually, not charges.

"You bet." Kayla nodded, chewing. Then she took out her phone again. A meme from Cerise. An ad for shoes and another for Kelowna real estate, of all things. Nothing from Zoe.

Message me, she wrote anyway. Again. Then she kept walking before the cold set in. By now she had learned it was best not to stop at all. That's when you got really cold. She ignored the blisters on her heels and continued towards Hearthstone. She wanted to check if Little Zoe was back.

She passed a construction site beside a mural depicting a wolf, ravens, salmon, and a grizzly. Not far from it were a crane and construction trucks, a blocked-off area and a sign with a glass high rise and SALES CENTRE – LIVE ABOVE IT ALL – CONDOS COMING SOON.

She passed by the consignment shop and a home décor store; in the window was a beautiful bed made up with a silky duvet and a sea of pillows. Not for the first time, Kayla stopped and stared, thinking of how wonderful it would be to sleep in it. She didn't steal and had never broken in anywhere, but nights when her leg really hurt, or when the weather was especially cold, she could imagine smashing that window and curling up under those soft duvets. On this morning, she could picture it well.

These days she saw places to sleep everywhere she went: in the pillowy curls of fabric at the base of Santa's sleigh in the holiday display a couple months back, that season when folks on the street made their own celebration singing carols and sharing discount pizza. She envisioned a place to sleep behind the metal grille that fenced off the doorway to the closed-down community college—if you could squeeze under that barrier you could sleep undisturbed. Yes, when she was tired enough, the world turned into places she might sleep. The city was too small to have any subways, so there were no warm subway grates to seek out like in movies, but she noticed awnings that could fend off the Okanagan's rain, and tucked-away spaces where you could fit just yourself and your pack. She saw places differently now.

Take that alley—it looked like just any alley with a dumpster. But so much happened there. Business got conducted, words got whispered or shouted, intimacies were shared and betrayed, friendships were made and broken, loves were lost or found, lives were taken and saved.

It was here in this alley that Cerise and Little Zoe would give each other shots in the mouth so there would be no needle marks to see on their arms—sometimes they thought of working indoors at a parlour where you had to look drug free. But most times they didn't plan that far ahead, going wherever they could find a vein.

And over there was the alley in which the older men would sit with their bottles and their cans, drinking whatever they had, beside them bags of collected empties so eventually they could go buy more. There was a community of those who drank, some the same folks each day and some who came and went, but everyone was welcome. Folks understood.

That was where Dan-o would tell his stories: his favourite was of teaching piano to kids. He'd been part of the 60s scoop that uprooted Indigenous kids from their families and put them into white homes to "civilize" them. The one good thing—the only good thing—he kept from being adopted out was that he learned to play the piano. And he did, every chance he got. He also told stories of hitchhiking across Canada and the States, playing gigs until he could no longer work. He skipped the details, but given his love of the bottle, Kayla could guess.

Dan-o was always saying how the weather was better down south, on the other side of the border that only some respected, but the life more cruel. How so many of the people he slept beside on the streets, or with whom he gathered around an oil drum fire, had seen war overseas and then gone on to live another war of their own upon return. And how down south there were so many children in the shelters—brimming shelters, which, like here, were not enough.

Just down from that alley where Dan-o spent his time was Eddie, his hoodie up, earphones on. His eyes were wild and he was saying something about how the dogs had messages for him.

"All the dogs are loud today," he was saying to Kayla and to all the street. She heard no dogs. But Eddie heard plenty of things others did not. He tried to keep the voices out, but his earphones didn't always work. Other times he said that they worked too well, with messages programmed for him. "They're telling us things. Can't anyone fucking listen?"

Kayla wanted to give him a hug, because everyone out here needed hugs, and Eddie sometimes especially, but he turned as abruptly as he'd come, and continued fuming down the street.

"Take care, Eddie," she said, mostly to herself.

She ignored her blisters and continued towards Hearthstone.

"Haven't seen her," the staff who opened the door said when Kayla asked about Little Zoe.

There was nothing to do except keep walking. Soon she'd head to the library, but it wasn't open yet. It was Sunday, which meant Habiba, the physics student, would be there studying. Habiba always shared the sweets she snuck in. *Knafeh*, those delicious rosewater pastries, meant *footprint of the heart* in the homeland her family had fled.

Kayla passed by Kori, who was spreading out a few pieces of clothing, a dish rack she must have salvaged from the trash, a half-empty bottle of cleaning solution, and a bag of day-old donuts.

"You want to buy anything?"

Kayla shook her head. But people did sometimes buy from Kori's pop-up shop—it was a way of getting things without going into a real store, where sometimes you got glared at. The dish rack and cleaning fluid, though, might be a tough sell. But finds were finds, and Kori was always game to try.

"You got a cigarette?" How many times had Kori asked, forgetting Kayla didn't smoke?

"You see Little Zoe anytime recent?"

Kori looked at Kayla with pupils already wide. "Bet I could think better if you went to the store and got me some smokes. I know you got cash on you, working girl."

"I don't have any smokes. When did you see her?"

"I maybe saw her last night?"

Kayla's hopes surged. "Last night? And?"

"Memory's a bit sketch, but I think it was last night. Went with some guy in a fancy-ass car."

"So you really think you saw her last night?"

"I think it was last night? Or maybe the night before?" Given how much she used, Kori's days and nights were known to blur.

"Which night was it? Think hard."

Kori just looked at her and raised her fingers to her lips, smoking an invisible cigarette.

"If I get you a fucking smoke can you remember? Anything? Plates?" Kori didn't memorize licence plates the way Kayla and her friends did. But just in case. "I'll see if anyone down the road has a smoke, okay? I'll bring one back if they do. You remember what kind of car?"

"I told you. Fancy ass. Black. Loud. Sweet and low."

Black—so not the Lamborghini.

"And you seriously can't remember if it was last night or the night before?"

"As I said." Then Kori turned away. She straightened the dish rack in front of her.

Kayla kept walking.

She passed City Pizza. It was owned by a guy named Bobby who treated folks out here just like anyone else. Not only would he let you linger inside to warm up, but he cooked special free pizzas on holidays, made sure everyone had something good happen that day no matter what. City Pizza was one business that never got its windows smashed.

Over there was the alley where she, Little Zoe, Cerise, and Lily had sat one night just weeks ago, after Little Zoe earned a huge tip and they all got Chinese New Year takeout. They ate fortune cookies and pored over the messages inside. *You will come into new knowledge,* Cerise's had said. *Your many talents will shine big and bright,* was Lily's. *You will meet someone who changes your life.* That one was for Little Zoe. *You are blessed with genuine friends,* Kayla's read, and, sitting in the alley, feasting in great company, she felt its truth.

And that alley over there, with its unassuming mouth—that alley was where Lily was raped by a pack of guys coming from the bar, laughing at her screams, saying you couldn't rape a hooker. That had been during the cold snap when many folks were in the shelters, so no one came running as they normally would. And Ketchum would have been out in the woods.

Not far from there, and on that same frigid night, someone else died on that stained sidewalk. Jim froze to death. All the shelters had been full. The media had called his death natural causes.

And there, over there, was where a yellow flower had bloomed last fall, emerging from between the bars of that rusted sewer, choked with refuse, a dandelion burst out radiant, despite.

"Look," Little Zoe had said, pointing the bloom out to Kayla. The plant's stem was long, as if it was reaching for light anywhere it could be found, and the flower was blooming bright. "Look," she repeated. "Just look."

Sunday, 8:30 a.m.

The morning traffic began to trickle into downtown. Kayla could smell bread wafting from bakeries. Crows ate last night's spilled fries from the sidewalk. Marta continued to knit. Gloria and Sally sipped their tea. Derek wrote in his notebook. Nelson gazed at the mountain's reflections in the lake as the day began to warm. There was still no sign of Zoe. No one had seen or heard from her.

Across the street was City Park, with its pathway along the water, the benches where Kayla sat sometimes. Kayla could see her favourite tree from here: a spruce with wide branches that stretched down to the ground and made a hiding place if you crawled under. Though she had to keep walking for now, to keep warm, to keep searching, it was her favourite place to go: right in the middle of the city, but hidden away from it all. She could crawl under there and just look up at the branches, streams of sunlight gleaming through, and be by herself. She would watch the birds going about their life, singing to each other or just to themselves, flitting from branch to branch, or just staying still, like her. Sometimes, if the night had been sleepless, she would curl up there by day, unseen. Protected under those branches, she could actually fall into a sleep deep enough to dream.

Though she hadn't told the others about it—that tree held something of a sacredness for her that she wanted to keep for herself—it had a name: *t'st'siɬp.* That was what Gloria called spruce in the nsyilxcən language she tried to keep alive in herself, refusing to be denied the shreds of her heritage. Gloria had taught Kayla that word, and more, in the woods at the base of Knox Mountain when she brought Kayla to collect herbs there once. Gloria had just lost her street daughter Cass to an overdose. That was before Sally came, and Kayla had been the only one around. As they had walked in the forest, surrounded by scrub bushes and trees stretching towards the sky, Gloria pointed at what they saw, saying their names in nsyilxcən. With the forest's overhanging branches and ravens calling above, Kayla couldn't tell if she felt like a guest or an intruder.

After they had collected the leaves, barks, and roots Gloria sought, she continued to share a few words, carving them into the dusty soil with a stick: *siya*—Saskatoon berry, *sʔatqʷɬp* – ponderosa pine, *t'st'siɬp*—spruce.

"I'm sounding these out for you because you grew up thinking what was written is real," Gloria had said, with a trace of anger in her voice. "And these—these are their real names I'm saying. I learned how to say them from my grandmother and aunties before I was taken away. But now I know how to write them too. And I want you to know their real names here in the Okanagan. Their real names."

Gloria had pointed upwards, past cottonwoods and aspens to the dark, verdant tops of pines. There, on a branch, was a raven, wings glistening a plummy black.

"See that raven up there? They're *yutəl'x*."

What Kayla had known as mountain, lake, forest, and deer all had first names. Gloria also taught her that rather than saying, "How are you?" it was truer to ask, *c'kin aspuʔus*—"How is your heart?" but only if you knew someone well and really wanted to know the answer. *Lim lemt*, Kayla was able to tell her, once she learned that word too. Thank you.

In honour of the origins of the tree she loved, in honour of the Okanagan land and its people, Kayla called the tree *t'st'siɬp*. And calling it by its real name, she loved it more.

But on this morning, as she walked through City Park, someone else was sleeping under that tree. She couldn't see them, but they had left their cart and bike outside. She would have liked to have tucked herself under those branches, to catch some sleep and some restoration, but the tree belonged only to itself and to the land, and someone else needed it now.

Not far from the shore's edge, she could see the park bench where she had slept when she first arrived in the city, seven months and forever ago.

When she had first reached the Okanagan, back in August, it had been a sweltering day. The window was down, the air rushing by as warm as an opening oven. She and Donna, the stranger who had driven her across five provinces for five days, crossed the bridge over Okanagan Lake at sunset. Kayla could still recall the speedboats pulling water skiers, party music and waves in their wake.

"You can come with me to the farm," Donna had said.

"No, I can't," was all that Kayla had been able to answer. She couldn't face another farm.

She had met the woman at a gas station on the night she'd had to leave. Kayla was drawn to the trailer hitched to the woman's truck, the horses' noses out the windows. Kayla overheard the woman telling a truck driver she was delivering horses to BC.

"Can I go with you?" Kayla had asked. That night she felt capable of anything.

The woman had looked at her hard, taking in her backpack, messy ponytail, and well-worn paddock boots. Kayla remembered hoping furtively that was all she saw.

"I need a ride. I can help pay for gas." Just barely.

The woman had kept staring. Kayla brought her hand to her mouth, hoped everything had been cleaned away.

"I'm Donna," the woman said, extending a hand. Kayla got the impression she was not one for many words, which was just what she needed right then.

In the truck, Kayla pretended to sleep. Through the fringe of her eyelashes, she caught Donna looking at her with something like recognition in her eyes. But Kayla had never seen the woman before, and the licence plate was from further east, which was partly why Kayla had approached her. She didn't want anyone to know who she was or where she had gone.

Northern Ontario had been a blur of pines out the window, insects splattering the windshield. Passing trucks had moose guards on their grilles. That first night they drove straight through, speeding into the dark, high beams flashing on the trees. Kayla watched everything rush behind her.

The second night they bedded the horses down at a layover barn. Donna was sleeping in the gooseneck, offered for Kayla to do the same, but Kayla preferred to stay in the truck, alone, keeping the windows up against mosquitoes. She stared out at the square of darkness and stars, past the dark silhouette of forest.

Manitoba was more trees and rivers until it became prairie. They stayed at a motel with a flyer for Victim Services at the front desk and on the bedside table. “We get a lot of girls from up north,” the hotel clerk said when she saw Kayla looking.

Donna made her sleep in a bed that night, saying the truck wasn’t safe here. In the motel room, Donna brought out beef jerky, but Kayla declined. Instead, she ordered a plate of fries at the motel diner, conscious of the money she was spending and wrapping some of the fries in a napkin to save for later. It was the first thing she had tried to eat since they left. She had to choke them down. She went to the diner mostly to get away from Donna—not because the woman talked but because her silence held the questions she wasn’t asking. Instead, Kayla picked at the fries, staring at hockey on the TV and avoiding the eyes of the only other patron, an elderly man who was slowly eating peas with a spoon.

Saskatchewan was endless fields—wheat, barley, oats, canola, flax, mustard, and lentils, lots of lentils, Donna told her. It was the first time they had spoken that day. Lentils. Kayla tried to calm herself by thinking of lentils, of anything but the night she left.

Big open fields stretched forever, as did a vast sky and rolling clouds. Wind rocked the trailer. Crossing towns, places with one flashing light at a single intersection, she thought of the farmland, how perhaps it was affordable for keeping horses. She wondered what her life would have been like if she had grown up here. She wondered what her life would be if she just got out of the truck. But she would stay for the full ride with Donna, as far as she would go.

Alberta erupted into swells of hills. Then came snow-capped mountains, jagged sky-high peaks. The Rocky Mountains were more gigantic than Kayla had ever imagined. Glacier lakes gleamed an impossibly bright pale blue. Wildflowers blazed on the hillsides, purple and orange and red. It would have been beautiful, had she wanted to see.

As they entered British Columbia, more mountains rose, but then their jaggedness smoothed. Eventually they reached the Okanagan, with its pines and rock bluffs and sagebrush. She tried to let her hopes swell along with the hills, as if she had finally come far enough.

When they reached Kelowna, Donna pulled over just after the bridge. Kayla thanked her again. Then she grabbed her pack and got out of the truck. She watched the lights of the trailer stream down the road, and breathed.

On the left of the highway was a park that bordered the lake: City Park, the sign read. Beyond its grassy, treed expanse was the water, where boats jetted by, some emanating music. Above the lake were mountains, sloping rather than steep, trees all the way to the top. Even at sunset, the sun was intense.

In the park she could see a playground, people playing beach volleyball. Teenagers preened in bikinis, gym-fit guys strutted without shirts, families took pictures with their phones. Between a colourful hotel and a low-rise, a cluster of people stood around smoking. A man in a fishing hat was ranting, while another was passed out on the sidewalk with a guitar; nearby was a bag lady with a cart. A guy on a bike, with a pit bull on a chain, was talking to a girl Kayla assumed was a hooker, from her sparkly mini dress and stiletto boots. Someone in uniform was there too, with a pad of paper. Kayla crossed the street, Leon Avenue, and kept going.

Further down, under trees at the park, a little girl was playing a brightly painted piano. Wafts from hotdog carts and food trucks, Thai and Ethiopian and poutine, drifted in the air. Seagulls and frisbees flew. Someone was selling sunglasses at a pop-up shop. A woman sold beaded dreamcatchers from outstretched arms.

Kayla continued towards a marina brimming with boats. As the road curved along the lake, it was busy with patio cafes. As people strolled by, trailing scents of pot and suntan lotion, she was conscious that she smelled of the barn. She hadn't wanted to take her clothes off to shower. She checked her hands again, reflexively, as she had caught herself doing repeatedly on the drive. But they were clean.

She saw a fridge of cold drinks through a window and realized that she was thirsty. She went into the first shop she saw, Ogopogo Giftland, filled with keychains and stuffed toys of a green serpent with a smile: the Ogopogo monster who lived in Lake Okanagan, according to the children's book on display. She reached towards one of the stuffed Ogopogos. It looked like a cartoonish version of the Loch Ness monster. Kayla would later learn from Gloria that, according to the Syilx people, the being in the lake was *nax̌aʔx̌aʔit*kʷ, a sacred being who protected the water.

But at that moment Kayla didn't know any of this, didn't know a thing about this new place, that it was considered a four-season paradise, with its lakeside resorts and world-renowned wineries, its hiking and biking in the hills and mountains, its skiing and snowboarding once winter's snow fell. She didn't yet know that it was a place where people worked hard and played harder. Where real estate prices were as high as the piercing blue sky, where hopes, dreams, and egos sailed and crashed, where pretty wasn't always beautiful and beauty only sometimes looked pretty.

At that moment, all she knew was that she was hungry as well as thirsty. She went into the fenced-off patio of one of the restaurants lining the sidewalk, a Mexican cantina pumping lively music. When the server in her black miniskirt came by, Kayla ordered a bean burrito platter with guacamole. It was a luxury and a foolish one too. She wasn't going to spend money like this often—far from it—but on this evening, this one summer evening, she would treat herself. Treat herself to the start of a new life.

She had come 4000 kilometres. She knew no one and no one knew her, or what she had done. She had no plans other than to be far away from where she had come. And she would have this, this one evening, before she would do whatever she had to do. As she always did.

*

That first morning in Kelowna, waking up on a City Park bench, with the sun just appearing above the mountains, she stirred to find a girl standing over her.

"Bylaw'll get you if you sleep here like that."

The girl was petite and tanned. She had big eyes and sores stippling her face, not quite acne. She was wearing a hoodie and a jean skirt, short enough to show a dragon curling up her thigh.

"Sorry?" Kayla sat up. From where she was on the park bench, the sun was beginning to shine on the water. Dew sparkled in the grass.

"Bylaw will be by soon. You can't just be sleeping there like that. Tourist season."

Kayla reached for her pack, which she had been using as a pillow. She began to mumble a thanks.

The girl stayed watching her. “You need someplace to sleep, I can tell you where some good places are.”

The girl stuck out her hand. Each of her fingernails was painted a different colour. “Little Zoe. People call me Little Zoe.” She smiled wide, revealing a grey tooth on one side. “Like I said, happy to show you a place where it’s alright to be.”

Before

Kayla had left the one place in her life where it felt alright to be.

The run-down townhouse she shared with her mother and her mother's string of boyfriends had never been that place. They moved there after her father died, trying out a succession of apartments and trailer homes where they never stayed long. Until Silvercreek Gardens. Kayla lived there for years, but it was never home.

Despite the name of the townhouse complex, the closest thing to a creek nearby had been the sewage tunnels across the highway. There were no gardens—only half-dead, scrubby bushes and tiny yards of browning grass and dog shit. Except for a few hopeful annuals one of the neighbours attempted, little grew.

And Kayla's mother's boyfriend—the one who came into their lives after Kayla's mother stopped crying and sleeping all day, the one who smiled and joked a lot, the one who paid the rent, the one who was nice enough to look after Kayla while her mother was at work, the one who was not the last but was the first, that one—didn't wait for Kayla to grow.

She could still feel the sting on her knees from the rough, grating fabric of that sofa. The sting on which she concentrated rather than the worse pain elsewhere. No, no, no, no, no, no. She had just concentrated on the sting on her knees as she stared into the fabric against her face, its coarse orange and brown weave, its fibres and its pulls, the way the threads went in and out. After, she saw the little stain on it that part of her had made. Where she had left her mark.

Not that her childhood was all bad.

There had been all those fuzzy, wonderful times with her dad when she was littlest, those days when her mother laughed a real laugh and hugged real hugs and didn't sleep so much and didn't say, *Be quiet, can't you just be quiet*, when Kayla didn't think she was being loud. But those days ended, and her dad was little more than a wishful fiction she clung to because she had so little else, save for one picture of them together: her in his arms, leaning against a car, both with such happy eyes. She had that photo in her backpack to this day, along with one of her grandma and one of Buddy.

And until she was six, when her mother got that one new boyfriend Kayla would refer to only as That One, Kayla's grandma had been there. She lived a couple of neighbourhoods away, in what was called The Ward, a working-class neighbourhood with Italian roots, though Kayla's grandma was not Italian, and lived there because it was one of the more affordable areas. Like her neighbours, she grew tomatoes, lettuce, and peppers in the well-tilled backyard she devoted to a garden. She'd left a small space unplanted, in which Kayla could play, a patch of dirt where Kayla could make mud pies and where dolls could have voices louder than just in her head.

Her grandma was a big woman with a big heart. She had grown up with little and tried to make up for Kayla's own version of little with lots of love and baking. Kayla could still taste her chocolate chip cookies when she thought of her. Her grandma had been there when her mother cried and slept all day after dad died, taking turns between her mother's bedroom and Kayla's own. *Everything is going to be alright,* she had said, hugging Kayla with her fleshy arms. And with her grandma it was.

Her grandma had been there for her on her first day of school and for runny noses and fevers. Weekends, the two of them would ride the bus downtown. They would go to the library and watch puppet shows and listen to story times. They would go to the bookstore that had a café inside, and after looking at the books together, Kayla savouring the pictures because sometimes the words jumbled together and reading came hard, they would sit in that café with hot chocolate or lemonade, looking out the window at the people going by. Kayla had no idea she was growing up poor because she wasn't. With her grandma, she had everything she needed, but when Kayla was six, her grandma died.

Her grandma always suspected the chemicals she used to clean people's houses had seeped into her body, and when the cancer came, she knew. She faded in increments, Kayla watching her grandma's ample body shrink along with her mind.

Kayla felt her world disintegrate too. She tried to have the dolls her grandma made console her. Kayla even let them speak outside her head, trying for words that could never do enough.

By the time her grandma actually stopped breathing, death seemed only a formality.

And so Kayla spent more time in the townhouse with her mother, staring at cartoons while her mother was at work, not opening the door for strangers and not eating any cookies. There were no longer cookies to eat. There was just a grandma-shaped hole in the universe. And, when Kayla's mother needed rent money and someone to look after Kayla, she got together with That One.

*

That One.

*

But Kayla found escapes.

That One could find her in the house, hiding in the kitchen cupboard behind the garbage pail, and he could find her in the neighbourhood, in a bush or under the porch, but he couldn't find her if she managed to hop on the bus.

After stealing change from her mother's bedside table (in nickels and dimes, so as not to be noticed—though money was tight and change mattered, so she must have noticed), Kayla would wait at the bus stop in agony, pleading the bus to come before he did.

She would go to the library that became a sanctuary, watching puppet shows and listening to story times by herself. She would go to the bookstore with the café that she now learned was called The Bookshelf, where she would lose herself in the pictures splashed in books of people's faces and places that could be far away, making up stories in her head about all the places she might someday go.

She would go to the Speed River, a real river, not like the sewage culverts across the highway from where Kayla lived. Plumes of bushes and cattails lined its banks. She would go to the The River Run Centre too, where she could sometimes hear strands of music from the back door.

But the place where she truly felt it was most alright to be—the one place that felt like the home she had always been waiting for—was the farm.

Before, Part Two

The farm Kayla loved wasn't fancy like the ones in magazines or the ones with perfect white fences around bright green paddocks, pristine barns. At age twelve, she'd seen a picture of it in the paper, with kids riding horses, and she wanted to be one of those kids.

From the road, it was just a red barn with peeling paint and split-rail fencing. A sign out front read: *Horse Boarding—Lessons—Summer Camps—Horses for Sale—Trail Rides.* But that farm was more than the place she took riding lessons, one hour a week in exchange for mucking stalls—an arrangement she made with the stable owner after biking there once she'd seen the picture.

That farm was more than where she learned to do barn chores. It was where she learned to lead a giant animal on a slack rope, the surprising trust despite the animal's power. Where she could move in unison with another being, no words required. Where she could breathe into the horses' necks as she brushed them, each stroke brushing away not only dirt and loose hair but whatever else needed to be brushed away. Where she learned how to help a child who had fallen get back on and where she learned not to fear her own voice when she raised it.

It was where she met friends who were her friends not because they were in the same grade or lived on the same street, but because they loved what she loved, and that was enough. These other girls spent all Saturday at the stables, too. The barn owner, Patricia, would let them stay all day if they made themselves useful: sweep the aisles, help the little kids tack up their ponies, scrub the water buckets, feed the hay.

Patricia let them know they were not to bother the ladies who boarded their horses at the stable, the ladies in their fancy breeches and tall boots or custom-made chaps, ladies whose horses had bridles with crystals on their browbands.

They also knew they were not to bother the live-in stable hand, Carl, after he retreated to his apartment beside the feed room once the dinner grain was fed. They were well aware, too, that they were not to pester John, Patricia's husband, when he came down to the barn from the big house to relax, pat the horses, or watch the lessons.

The girls watched the lessons too. They studied Demi Ray, the trainer people paid to ride their horses and develop their potential. *Heels down. Sit up, shoulders back. Inside rein to outside leg. Eyes looking where you want to go.*

The girls wanted to be her. They would stand by the riding ring, watching her teach lessons, ready to lend a hand, do up the girth or put the bridle on. They were there to do anything that needed doing, to soak in all things horse. They called themselves the Barn Junkies—the BJs for short—before they thought of other things those initials might mean.

The BJs took the bottle of gentian violet used to clear up ringworm infections and took turns streaking their own hair bright violet. (Even out west, Kayla dyed the tips of her hair violet.) They drank straight from the hose out back when they were thirsty. For lunch, they would go to the pub at the golf course across the road. Those who had a bit of spending money in their pockets—pockets that inevitably also had half a carrot, a piece of bailer twine, or braiding yarn—would order a basket of fries to share. The servers at the golf course hated them, this flock of dirty girls who were boisterous and never tipped. But the manager overlooked their hay-flecked hair and the mud on their boots, noticing how some patrons didn't mind the girls in their tight breeches, the newness of their hips. But the BJs did not dwell on such attention, or perhaps even notice it. They would go back to the barn and set up courses of jumps with poles in the outdoor ring, turn themselves into horses and canter around, not afraid to soar in the air.

The girls all had their favourite horse or pony, the one who got smuggled handfuls of grain from the feed room, the last carrot. For Kayla that horse was Buddy. He was swaybacked and had the thin, upside-down neck of a ewe. His plain brown coat was dull and marked with scars from bites and barbed wire. His thin tail never seemed to grow long. He had an overbite. But his eyes were beautiful and kind.

When she rode him she was transported from where she was. Everything else in the world fell away. All that mattered was that moment. She barely saw the dirt path in front of her, the blur of all beside—just his ears and view beyond, the openness of the sky above. Nothing could catch her. She did not think of anything, except that she was here and she was strong and she was free.

She savoured her one sanctioned hour of riding per week, and she snuck in extra rides, too. When she saw Patricia's truck pull out of the driveway, she would slip Buddy out of his stall, put his bridle on, and climb onto his back. They would go past the manure pile, past all the paddocks and the final fence, and into the woods beyond. That forest kept getting smaller as bulldozers from the not-so-distant subdivision encroached, paving the way for houses where the woods once grew. But there were enough trees to get lost in. Kayla always let Buddy choose the way.

On one of those journeys, Kayla took Buddy to Burger King, nudging him towards the drive-thru.

"Welcome to Burger King. What can I get for you today?" the crackly voice asked before they must have realized she was not in a car.

"Large fries," she replied.

"You're on a horse!" came the voice.

She fed Buddy the fries in the parking lot, still on his back, his neck curving towards her and his big teeth gentle as she held out each one.

A man who looked homeless approached. He appeared rumpled and used up, with bony cheeks. She wondered if she should give him some fries.

"Can I pet your horse?" he asked instead.

Her horse. If only. But in a way, he was.

When she nodded, the man patted Buddy, then buried his face in Buddy's neck.

She relaxed the reins, let him take whatever time he needed.

*

One day, Buddy was crying in one eye.

The vet was out to the barn that day, to see one of the boarder's horses, and Kayla begged her to look at Buddy. The vet examined his eye, nearly swollen shut, and diagnosed a corneal abrasion. A bad one that could cost Buddy his sight.

The future for a horse with vision problems at a lesson barn wasn't good. Buddy would have to have special ointment put in his eye every two hours, but Patricia wouldn't pay to treat an old school horse.

Kayla, teary, asked the vet how much it cost. "I'll do anything I can."

"I think I have some ointment that's just expired, but it'll do the trick."

Kayla put the ointment in Buddy's eye just as the vet instructed. She slept on the bales outside of Buddy's stall. Thankfully it was summer, but she would have missed school, fought with her mother, done anything to stay. But her mother was having issues with her boyfriend—a new boyfriend, long past That One—and said it would be all right. She had her own life and seemed grateful that Kayla was getting hers.

On the first night Kayla was caring for Buddy, John came down from the big house. She had just pulled Buddy from his stall and was getting the ointment ready.

"Here, let me help you," he said, coming towards her.

Kayla tensed. Something seemed off.

"I'm good. I've got it," she told him, using that bigger voice she had only found at the barn. She grabbed her phone. "I've just been talking with the vet. She's phoning me back any second." Kayla held the phone up as if garlic to a vampire.

"Alright then," John said, turning with a shrug. "Patricia just wanted me to check on you. See if you needed help. But if you've got it...well, have a good night."

She stayed still, like an animal trying to go undetected, until she heard the barn door close. Then, breathing heavily, she buried her face in Buddy's neck.

Kayla kept nursing Buddy. His eye opened wider by the next day and eventually stopped crying.

That was the summer that Buddy started nickering to her. Most of the horses nickered in the morning when she rolled out the feed cart, but even a teenage girl knew it was for breakfast rather than for her. But all she had to do was walk into the barn, any time of day, and Buddy started nickering to her for real. If he were outside in his paddock with the rest, he would see her and trot or canter over, and would stand there as she stroked his face.

That was the summer Kayla bought her own paddock boots with the money she had saved from babysitting, raking leaves, and shovelling snow from driveways. She had been getting by with a pair of threadbare breeches (a gift from a parent at the stable whose child had outgrown them) and rubber rain boots. But as soon as she saved enough, she had biked to the tack store.

Willow Equestrian smelled of leather tack and horse feed. She bought a pair of paddock boots just like the other girls had, like the ones that made Demi Ray look so professional. And she wore those boots everywhere, so proud. In time, they softened, became molded to her feet. They became hers.

That was the summer a boy started coming to the barn, one with his own horse. Some of the BJs wrote his name, Sebastian, with their own in the arena dirt with the heel of their boot. Kayla noticed that some of them started wearing tighter tops when he was around. They practiced sitting trot, or no-stirrup riding, their chests bobbing under the thin fabric. Not Kayla.

That was the summer Carl started calling Kayla by her name as he took care of the horses, unloaded the hay, repaired the fences. After work he retreated to his apartment beside the feed room, from which they heard strains of sad country music and the occasional clink of glass. He wore a belt buckle that he said he won competing rodeo back in the day. He didn't speak much, but when he did, any story or piece of advice was accompanied by *back in the day.*

"You can tell a good horse by whether they roll all the way over," Carl would tell her. "Or from how they drink. A good horse sticks their nose full in, not just lips touching the surface."

Carl called all the BJs "Missy" and left them to go about their business as long as they left him to go about his. He always carried around a travel mug of coffee, but if you got close, you could tell from his breath it was more than coffee.

She once overheard Carl talk back to the farrier as he was shoeing the horses. The farrier was saying that he liked both his horses and his women to start off wild and then get well broke, his way. Carl's voice had been unusually cold. "That's no way to talk of ladies," he said. "Have some respect."

Carl knew that Kayla was feeding Buddy extra hay, and grain pilfered from the feed room, but never said a word. He caught her once, coming back from her adventures in the forest past the fences, and her face must have paled with her secret.

"I ain't telling no one," Carl said, leaning in the door jamb of his apartment. She tensed, but he left her alone with the horses and closed the door behind him, wanting nothing in return.

That was the summer that Kayla started to tell some of her secrets. She listened to the other girls in the hayloft, their hushed whispers, but she told her own secrets only to Buddy as she brushed him. He listened to everything, especially the things that had no words.

It took more years before she moved into that tiny apartment beside the feed room, but that was the summer Kayla knew she was home.

Sunday, 7:30 p.m.

"I need some smokes before we get going." From the way Cerise was pacing, Kayla could tell her friend needed more than cigarettes. But to afford her fix, she had to work first.

Kayla and Cerise had been walking down Leon towards their usual corner, but swung towards Safeway for Cerise's smokes. In the grocery store's parking lot, sitting in a car and facing the food store's brick wall, was a woman they knew—Livia. She was one of the outreach volunteers, the one who gave Kayla her sleeping bag when she was new in town, the one who gave Little Zoe the unicorn necklace along with a golden locket that her friend had tucked away. *I'm saving this for something special,* Little Zoe had said.

Every evening, the outreach volunteers would come to give out hotel-sized soaps and shampoos, warm clothes, condoms, clean needles, Naloxone kits. Some even brought used makeup and jewellery. They also shared chocolate and candy. Not everyone on the street wanted to talk with them, but candy helped. The organization's founder raided Walmart for Halloween candy every November first. The organization also kept a record of bad dates the girls reported—clients who mistreated, refused to pay, or worse. Of course, those on the streets had their own ways of letting each other know, but the volunteers could be a go-between to talk to the police if anything happened. Most folks on the streets didn't trust cops.

But Livia was early today. Kayla was surprised to see her just sitting there in the cold, staring at the wall and sipping from a travel mug. Then she reached for something beside her—a wine bottle. She poured some wine into the travel mug and kept sipping.

"Looks like Livia's getting the party started," Cerise remarked, but the look on Livia's face was far from celebratory.

"Everyone's got something."

Safeway was nice and warm. As they stood in line for Cerise's cigarettes, Kayla could feel the glare of the woman behind them.

With Kayla in her tiny kilt and Cerise in her stilettos, they were dressed for a night of work, and Kayla's backpack, sleeping bag rolled on top, was far from convincing anyone she went to school. Cerise glared right back at the woman and swung her hips a little more than usual as she left.

Kori was already in the parking lot when they came out. Kayla could see her beside Livia, who was bent over the trunk of her car, stuffing hats, mitts, and clothes into a bag. Though Kayla thought she was about thirty, the weariness on her face made her look older. Kori was taking the items out of the bag as soon as Livia put them in, checking out the wares.

A Toyota pulled up beside Livia's. It was Wanjiru, one of the other volunteers, with her many long braids curled on top of her head into a bun. Wanjiru was a nursing professor, but when she had first arrived from Kenya she had worked as a nurse in a jail. She was the best volunteer to consult with on any health problem—the walk-in clinics were so busy—and she was there for other matters too. She had been there for Gloria after her daughter overdosed; she had helped Lily after her rape; she had helped Cerise research organizations advocating for safe working conditions for sex workers. She also had a strong bullshit detector.

In addition to the chocolates, protein bars, water, and juice boxes the volunteers handed out—the juice boxes making those on the street look like displaced kids during a school lunch—Wanjiru brought hot home-cooked meals. Wrapped in tinfoil to keep them warm, Wanjiru brought tastes of comfort she'd known in Kenya: *nyama choma* and stodgy *ugali*, maize meal porridge that stuck to your ribs like oatmeal. She also brought *sukuma wiki*, cooked greens that meant "pushing the week" in Kiswahili. You ate them when you had money for nothing else, she said. *And they are so good for you*, Wanjiru reminded them more than once. She worried that those on the street didn't get enough vegetables.

Folks appreciated the food. A few also appreciated the tinfoil it was wrapped in. They used it to cook their heroin.

"Evening," Wanjiru greeted. She began pulling out her own bags of supplies. "How are you doing? How many Naloxone kits you got tonight?"

"Enough, I hope. And I'm good." Livia's voice reminded Kayla of her own when she said she was fine sometimes. But she *was* good. Kayla liked that Livia made an effort to learn what folks out here not only needed but wanted: she knew all their sizes and would bring clothes that fit, rather than just whatever topped the pile of donations in the organization's storage shed. She knew Mama B liked purple, Cerise was partial to sexy and sparkly, that the girl who sang the ABC song couldn't tolerate itchy tags. She cleaned the donated jewellery she curated from the storage unit. Boiling it with baking soda and vinegar returned the shine, she said. Kayla could remember the look on Little Zoe's face when Livia had given her the unicorn necklace and the locket, the rare smile that Livia had given in return.

"I need shampoo, conditioner. Body lotion. Toothpaste. A toothbrush. A hairbrush too," Kori was rattling off. "Condoms, cleans. And what clothes are there? Any makeup? Perfume?"

Lily and Sally were also waiting there by now. Kayla and Cerise let them go ahead, since Cerise was finishing her smoke. Sally was dotting soy sauce on a tray of sushi. A nearby sushi place handed out what they hadn't sold at closing the day before it expired. *But it's always still good,* Little Zoe had assured Kayla when she first arrived in town. When Little Zoe had offered Livia and Wanjiru sushi one night, Livia had seemed flattered, as though finally being accepted.

"How's your night going?" Lily asked Livia and Wanjiru, both her smile and pupils wide.

"Going well," Wanjiru answered. "How are you? You keeping warm enough? Need anything?"

"I wouldn't say no to mittens. And a few Band-Aids and alcohol wipes if you've got any." Lily moved her arm up and down, as if flapping a heavy wing. "This arm. Infected again."

Lily's arm had gotten swollen and purple this past autumn, nasty at the vein where she injected most. It needed more than a Band-Aid.

Livia rummaged in her bag. Some of the volunteers kept their supplies neatly organized, ready to dispense quickly, but Livia kept hers less organized on purpose. Kayla had overheard her and Wanjiru talking about how taking the time to look for something meant more time to talk. More than supplies and harm reduction kits, sometimes it was the conversation, the connection, the respect, that people sought most. That harm reduction.

"I could use a warmer coat," Sally added. "If you've got one."

Livia handed her one. It was nice. Kayla wondered if it had once been Livia's. Some volunteers, like Livia and Wanjiru, commandeered some of their own items when supplies ran low. Livia once admitted she brought a dress she liked because someone out here would appreciate it more.

"Thanks so much." Sally waved the tray of sushi around, offering the last one. Then she pulled the coat on over her thin jacket.

Next came Alexa in her size twelve platform boots, her special necklace glittering under the streetlights. Her phone was playing a faint song. She liked to make music wherever she went.

"If you have any foundation, I'd really appreciate it." But it wasn't just stubble she sought to hide, this time. Kayla saw the bruise across Alexa's cheek. She'd heard that it was from a john who'd grown angry at what he'd done and with whom.

Alexa reached to her face, the purpling of her bruise.

"You know," Wanjiru said, "we have resources we can connect you with—"

"Hey!" came a loud voice from across the parking lot. It was Teflon, in her Raiders coat and baseball cap, hood pulled over top, riding a too-small bike, with stubs where a child's streamers had been cut from the handlebars. The bike was back.

"You have any new clothes tonight?" Teflon grabbed a hoodie sticking out of one of the bags. She draped it over her arm, even though she must have seen it would be too small. Most folks didn't take what they wouldn't use or couldn't give to someone they knew. But Teflon was not most folks, Kayla thought. Teflon took what she could, when she could. But she also had her kindnesses. When she was looking after Jason's pit bull, Blaze, while her friend was in jail, she made sure Blaze was warm at night. She had even taken him to one of the big box pet supply stores along the highway and cruised the treat aisle, Blaze helping himself to biscuits, rawhide, bones.

Then Marta was there with her cart. She reminded Kayla of her grandma. "Just socks. I just really need some dry socks," Marta was saying. Street feet, from staying in wet shoes, were the worst. In winter the wetness would freeze. Marta wasn't the first to lose toes.

Then came the girl they always saw, but who never gave her name. Kayla didn't know where she stayed. The girl, thin and wary of looking anyone in the eye, just appeared. Despite her silence, her hesitancy, the girl got into cars in the evenings, somehow. Kayla had seen that.

The girl wondered if there was any underwear.

I'm very broken down there, she had once whispered to Kayla, but she had said no more. On this night, she walked away, wordlessly, as soon as Livia handed her what she had asked for.

"Hey," Wanjiru said, turning to Kayla and Cerise. "Thanks for waiting. How are you two doing?"

"We're good," Cerise answered. "Just having a birthday party for Naomi 'til the cops came by."

"Fuckers," sighed Wanjiru. Her teenage son had already been harassed by police. "Well, I'll have to wish Naomi a very happy birthday when I see her." She noticed Cerise was shuffling foot to foot. "You need anything?"

"Respect? Housing? Safety? Decriminalization?" Cerise laughed, though not exactly laughing.

Wanjiru nodded in solidarity.

"There is something," Kayla found herself saying. "I haven't seen Little Zoe in two days."

Livia and Wanjru's eyes widened.

"Have you gone to the police?" Livia asked.

"I figured she'd just come back. But she hasn't texted me back. And that's not like her. Not for this long."

"Sometimes she just goes incommunicado, though," Cerise added. "Wouldn't be the first time."

"Shit, though." Wanjiru's face was stone. "Do you want to talk to the cops? Or Livia and I could to go to the station as soon as we're done outreach?"

"The cops won't do anything," Cerise scoffed. "Not for one of us."

"I'm sure they'll do all they can," Livia said.

"I'll let everyone on the outreach chat forum know to look out for her," said Wanjiru. "We can make posters. Alerts. Get the word out. Can you give any details?"

It was all happening so fast—Kayla had just assumed Little Zoe would be back. But when she saw the concern in the women's faces—especially Wanjiru's, since Wanjiru didn't rattle—she felt that sickening worry deepen.

"When did you see her last?" Wanjiru asked.

"Friday. We just went out to work like any night. Nothing unusual. I don't know what dates she went on. One of the other women said she saw her get in a black sports car, but she wasn't sure what night that was."

Livia had her phone out, recording everything Kayla could tell her. "Can you give us a description of her we can give the police? I mean, we know her, but you know her better." Kayla could smell the wine on Livia's breath, but she didn't seem drunk at all.

"She's twenty. Not even five feet tall. Tiny. She has long blonde extensions. Dark brown eyes."

"The other night she was wearing a purple miniskirt and thigh-high black boots," Cerise added. "And a black coat."

"And she would have had a black hoodie on underneath," Kayla continued. "One with these sparkly designs on it. Like angel wings. With glitter. And she's got a missing tooth at the side. A dragon tattoo on her thigh..."

But what description could feel sufficient for someone Kayla had come to love so dearly, in a world where such love was rare?

Sunday, 11:00 p.m.

"So we have to be discreet," the man driving said, again. He had picked Kayla up looking both sheepish and excited. When she'd told him how much, he didn't scoff at the price. She'd made it a good one, given the newness of his Escalade. He had Kayla sit in the backseat, where there were tinted windows. He didn't want anyone to see her. There were two children's car seats, one with high-contrast infant toys. She pretended she was in the back of a limousine, being driven. She hadn't stopped feeling worried for Little Zoe, but the necessity of work had a way of eclipsing such feelings, of distracting, even just for a while.

They left the downtown and went up Lakeshore Road, as if heading to the dog beach, but kept going. They passed orchards and a winery, but then the area turned residential. The storybook houses had columns and wrap-around porches, trees planted in symmetrical patterns, and detached garages bigger than the townhouse in which Kayla had lived at Silvercreek Gardens.

"They filmed a movie up here last year," the man said. "A Christmas movie. Hallmark Channel."

"Nice." With yards bright with snow, the houses big and perfect, Kayla could picture it as a movie set. A snowman in a jaunty scarf graced one of the yards; another house had a giant inflatable heart: *Happy Valentine's.* She could imagine all the perfect families who lived here, their lives as shiny as their new SUVs, their dreams as big and pretty as their houses.

She was chronicling it all in her head. She would have to tell Little Zoe about it later. She could practically hear Little Zoe advising her, *Really work this one, girl.* This man would hopefully tip well. Kayla would see to it that he did. He might be generous to keep her quiet; he might be the sort to buy her gifts. Little Zoe had taught her all the signs, and, as he continued chatting nervously, winding through the neighbourhood, he satisfied the whole list.

Eventually they came to a part of the subdivision that was just being built, with some houses just frames or only half finished.

Real estate agents' signs were staked in the front yards, which were just dirt naked of sod. Mud showed through the patches where snow had melted.

"My wife and kids are at her sister's," the man explained as they pulled into the garage of a house that looked more like an office building than a home.

After he'd skulked inside the garage, she grabbed for her pack, with her sleeping bag rolled on top. He looked at her as she slung it over her shoulder.

"Well, let's go inside, then," the man said awkwardly, as if reassuring himself.

The garage was big, with two ATVs, a hockey net, skis hanging on the walls. He led her into a mudroom that opened into a kitchen. When he flicked on the light, she could see granite counter tops, a giant brushed steel fridge. Everything was gleaming. A single takeout container sat on the counter, holding gristle from a steak.

"Let's have a drink," the man said before his coat was off. He reached into a cupboard, grabbed a bottle, and poured two full glasses. He motioned towards a leather sectional in the living room. His hand on her leg like a stage prop, he clinked their glasses.

"Cheers."

She pretended to take a sip.

"So...are you saving up for college?" Before she could answer, he continued. "I know a girl like you who saved up for college doing this. Adrianna was her name. Pretty girl. You know her?"

Kayla did not, though she knew more than ever that she would put on a special show tonight, in case this man made a practice of helping women out. She had heard of girls, and some guys, who paid for living expenses and even tuition this way, with a sugar daddy or two or three on the side. Kayla had heard rumours of a woman who became a successful accountant and now had a condo overlooking the lake, and a BMW, though Kayla had never met these people personally.

That's how you do it, Cerise said some nights. From her stories, Vancouver had been close to that life for her too, at least in the early days—though something in her eyes suggested not quite.

"I'd love to go to university," Kayla told the man. For tonight it could be true. It would have been even truer if the words on the page could stop from jumbling together every time she tried to read.

"Yeah. University would be great," she tried again. If she ever went back to school, she could get someone to read to her, help her out. Cerise had been to college for a year, and said such things were possible. But further schooling had never been the plan for Kayla—not just because of her dyslexia but because she hadn't been raised to think that way. Her mother made it clear that school was something to endure, just like her work as a server. And in school she'd heard what the teachers weren't saying: she wasn't the type to make it to college or university.

The man just took another drink and stroked her on the thigh. "I have an idea for us tonight."

She wondered what it was that his wife wouldn't let him do.

"Tell me," Kayla told him, looking him in the eye.

He smiled. He must have thought he controlled the narrative, sipping his fine drink in his fine house, thinking he had bought a woman for the evening.

Rented, not bought, Little Zoe always clarified. *As if you could even begin to have all of me!*

"Or shall I tell you?" Kayla was surprised at the assuredness of her own voice.

Little Zoe would be proud.

This was not the life she had envisioned, but she had known what she was doing when she started this work—as much as anyone could. Or so she told herself. She hadn't been tricked into it, bullied or coerced. She knew she had something of value; she'd known that since she was a little girl. If it was something to be taken or used for free, she might as well earn a living.

Later, as she moved above him, feeling his body transform because of her, listening to the breathing that was all because of what she was doing, what she could do, she knew that for a thin sliver of time, she was the one who held the power.

*

The first man Kayla ever went with was someone Little Zoe had gone with before. He was safe, she said. He didn't bargain, and he would never take his money back—something Kayla didn't yet know to fear. He liked to sample what was new.

He had picked her up in a silver Audi. He was fortyish, glasses, looked very normal. He didn't look like the psychology professor Little Zoe said he was. She had pictured someone in a suit, perhaps with leather patches at the elbows. This man had Birkenstocks, reflective sunglasses, and a knowing smile.

She remembered looking at her own face in the reflection of those sunglasses, wondering how he saw her. Wondering who she was. Who she was about to be.

But she would do what she had to do, what she had dared herself to do. She felt she had nothing to lose.

She had originally thought that she should dress for the occasion—if she were going to do this, shouldn't she look the part? But Little Zoe said this man preferred not to draw attention. He had once asked Little Zoe to take off her makeup. He had even bought her a hoodie, the one with the glittery angel wings she always wore, to cover up her skimpy dress.

When Kayla started to envision actually going with clients, she had intended to borrow something to wear from Little Zoe, put on a different outfit for this different version of herself. But Little Zoe insisted: this man liked it when a girl looked like she needed a bit of help.

The man took her to a pub on Leon. Not the place with the OPEN sign lit with just the E, where folks from the street sometimes splurged on a drink and some warmth, but a sports bar further up, Tonics. Hockey was on the big TVs. People sat at the bar with pints. A chalkboard advertised that the soup of the day was cream of broccoli, that there was a special on burgers and primavera. She didn't know what she had thought this would be, but somehow this was not what she had imagined.

She watched the server bring a tray of drinks to the group beside them. Then she stared at the packs of sugar in a container beside the ketchup, at the grain of wood in the table.

"Are you hungry?"

He motioned for the server, who looked at him rather than Kayla. "A striploin and a Heineken. For both of us."

"I don't eat meat," Kayla said quietly and too late. The server was already heading for the kitchen. But then Kayla thought of the dead flesh ready to be consumed, prepared as if pretty, with mashed potatoes on the side. She thought of how this man might see her: flesh ready for consumption. She was not that. Refused to be that. Not anymore, not like That One had made her feel. No. She would not be that flesh.

"I'll have the primavera," she called to the server. When she didn't seem to be heard, Kayla stood and raised her voice a bit louder. "Primavera, please."

She sat back down, looked at the ketchup and sugar packets and the tempting grain of wood, the strange comfort it offered.

"So Desiree," the man said—Little Zoe had said to choose a name—"what do you like to do?"

What did she like to do? Her life had become built around survival, not choice. Not that she needed to explain anything thing to him. She knew what she loved to do, what she used to love to do. But he didn't deserve to know that. "I spend time with friends, and I walk a lot," Kayla said finally, looking him in the eye. "I walk and I look at things and..."

When his mouth curled up in slight amusement, she realized that how she spent her days was not what he meant.

"So you're a *flanneur,*" he said then. "Someone who strolls. An observer of modern urban life."

"I walk. And I like to look at the world around me."

The server came by with the beers. From her look, it was clear she knew that Kayla was underage but also that it was too late. Or perhaps she would have served her anyway. There was something like sympathy in her eyes.

But Kayla didn't feel she needed sympathy. Having heard the conviction in her own voice, having the courage to look this man right back in the eye, she was starting to feel the beginnings of a new strength.

The man raised his glass. She kept hers where it was. She didn't drink—her mother's love affair with Jack Daniels had destroyed the romance of drinking before it began, and besides, she knew she needed to stay present, to keep her wits about her. For once, she needed to be the one in control. She pushed the beer away. "Yes. I like to take in the world around me."

*

In the hotel, she did what she had come to do. But she did more too. As he moved above her, and then as she had moved above him—she had surprised him, and herself, by climbing on top—she did not leave her body as she was used to doing.

She did not stare at the texture of the sheets, immersing herself in that fabric as she knew how to do, the fabric that might as well have been the weave of an orange and brown plaid couch. She did not disappear into that fabric. No.

She refused to lose herself or disappear.

And as she moved above him, she moved in a way that she had never moved before. Though this was the first time since That One—but not what she thought of as her First Time—she decided she hadn't had that yet—she realized she did not have to lie helpless, or vacate herself, or to be what she was expected to be.

She realized that she could be something—*someone*—other than that scared little girl.

No. She did not have to go about this as she feared. What she was doing was far from ideal and far from what she had dreamed, if she had dreamed that way at all—she had been so young when it happened that she'd never had a chance to develop a fantasy of her own, before it was contaminated—but it was something. There was something in staying present—something unexpected, compromised, unideal—but *something*—as she heard the sound of her own breath and realized that she was there. After all she had been through, all she had endured and suffered in silence, she was still there. Breathing and filling up the room with her presence, despite it all.

Monday, 2:00 a.m.

Finished her work for the night, Kayla stepped into the cold and started down the dim street. She could see the outlines of half-built houses further down the road, framed in wood, the night sky visible through the gaps between the beams.

The man had offered to drive her back downtown—she got the impression he wanted to get her both out of his neighbourhood and his conscience—but she'd said no. After they had come down from the bedroom upstairs—the upstairs of the house sparsely furnished with cheap furniture, as if the main floor had been for show—he'd ended up having plenty more to drink. She didn't want him to drive her anywhere. And this picture-perfect movie-set neighbourhood was worth exploring.

None of the housing sites were fenced. She could just walk inside, entering someone's house but not necessarily through the door. Her footsteps echoed on the naked plywood floor. Nothing was finished. There were no pipes or wiring yet roughed in. The rooms inside were framed up, but not yet with solid walls. The part of the roof that was built so far was unshingled wood. But it was enough.

She sat in someone else's future house and pulled out her phone. *Write to me. You would have been proud of me tonight.* She meant it less as a need for approval than a shared camaraderie. *Please write.* Then, as she sat there, trying not to worry, starting to imagine what it would be like to live here in this storybook neighbourhood, she realized she was tired. She also realized this would be a great place to stay. So she unrolled her sleeping bag, layered up her clothes for warmth, and crawled inside.

She could see the twinkling valley of the city, the amber-lit stripes of roads stretching toward downtown. She could see the dark curve of the lake, the west side beyond. Whoever lived in this house would have quite the view. For now, it was hers.

Burrowing further into her sleeping bag, alone and safe and appreciative of all she could see, she recalled another time she had seen the city from afar: that day Little Zoe had brought Kayla to Dilworth Mountain back in autumn. Kayla had been exhausted by her new life, by the need to be constantly alert, the relentless logistics of mere survival, the way people looked at her. The way she looked at herself.

"Come with me," Little Zoe had said. "You need a different view. You can see so far from up there."

They had set off from downtown when the sun was high. It was early evening before they reached the top. Kayla's bad hip and leg had complained, but she did not. Little Zoe brought apples; it was harvest time in the Okanagan, and Marcel had brought some to share. Everyone on Leon had apples that day. He had shared some of the best with Kayla and Little Zoe.

Little Zoe took Kayla up winding streets with large houses, manicured lawns, and mature trees. They came to a park, with a swing set and a slide, before the trails began. A little girl in pigtails was there, playing, with a woman looking on. Little Zoe paused. When she saw the girl's face, her body relaxed—or deflated. Perhaps both.

"Let's swing," Little Zoe said finally, pulling Kayla over to the swing set. And so they swung, flying higher and higher, hair streaming in their faces, feeling a freedom neither had felt so much as children, laughing at the surprise and sheer glee.

When the sun started to melt into the mountains, Little Zoe led Kayla down a trail surrounded by ponderosa pine and tall cottonwoods, sprays of purple asters, wild daisies and goldenrod. Pine trees clung to the side of a steep, rocky hill that overlooked the city.

Little Zoe was right about the views—you could see the city from all these different angles: curved streets of neighbourhoods, kidney-shaped pools, swathes of agricultural land. There was the highway, the mall and the hospital, big-box stores and car dealerships, and a large building Little Zoe said was a juice factory. Kayla could even see downtown, with its cluster of high-rises, its cranes to build more.

They passed hikers and people walking dogs. Dressed as Kayla and Little Zoe were, with no hint of work on them, they could have been students out for a hike. Tourists even. Or people who lived in this pretty neighbourhood.

Up on Dilworth Mountain that day, Kayla had wondered what it would be to be elsewhere, how others would see her when she was just herself. But just herself—what was that, now? She had asked herself that a lot since the night she left Ontario.

Kayla and Little Zoe had sat there as evening became dusk, taking in the view, eating apples. Kayla hadn't felt such peace since the farm. She was struck by how different it was from being immersed in the close-up grime of the city, the grit of day-to-day survival. How another world was possible.

"Want to see something else?" Little Zoe eventually asked, turning to Kayla.

"Sure."

Little Zoe led Kayla through the darkened park. She took her down the street of nice big houses and stopped in front of one with a sweeping garden, a wrap-around porch, and a large oak. A light shone through closed Venetian blinds. There was a picket fence that separated off the backyard, which had a playhouse, picnic table, sandbox, a polka-dot ball. In a toy stroller lay a doll, carefully tucked into blankets, with its own little bear for company.

"This is where my daughter lives," Little Zoe finally said.

*

The week after Little Zoe took Kayla up Dilworth Mountain, Nelson pulled Little Zoe's tooth. It was infected and interfering with her work. For weeks, she'd been holding her jaw, taking drugs like medicine. Even Nelson, who usually kept his distance as he binned for empties and drank alone, had noticed. That day Little Zoe had been crying. Thinking it was the tooth—perhaps hoping it was the tooth, because that was something fixable—Nelson abandoned his usual routine and offered.

"I've done this before," he said, "in the field."

It was a rarity that he spoke of his past. Out here, many folks just stuck to the present moment. Everyone was respectful of that. There was an unspoken rule that the past was not to be scratched into unless someone scratched there first themselves. For Nelson, the only glimmer into who he had been was this mention of the field—and the one night he had used the word *too.*

He used the word *too* after a man took him to the pub one morning after seeing him on the street. No one knew why the man had chosen Nelson, other than such a thing happened to some folks out here, every so often: they could get a pint or two when someone walking by was especially lonely and wanted to buy an ear. Dan-o, ever thirsty and jealous of such an invitation, later said there must have been something about Nelson that pegged him. Maybe they even knew each other from before. Either way, Nelson and the man were gone for hours. Nelson returned quiet as always and with a 40-ouncer of Jim Beam. About the other man he said only, *He fought in Afghanistan too.* Nelson drank by himself that night, as usual, but they had all noticed the *too.*

"Pull it. That's what I need to do," Little Zoe had told Nelson. She stared at him solidly through tears.

Earlier that day Little Zoe had planned to see her daughter. Kayla now knew that she had two daughters: a baby in foster care in Victoria and a five-year-old who lived with foster parents in Kelowna. Both daughters had been taken by the Ministry of Children and Family Development. Little Zoe was allowed to see her five-year-old daughter two weekends per month, supervised. This development was new, and had to do with Little Zoe meeting some condition. Kayla respected certain silences and the importance of not asking too many questions.

All morning the day of the visit, before Little Zoe asked Nelson to pull her tooth, she had waited. She talked about wishing she had craft supplies, to have something special to share with her child. She got ready at Hearthstone, as usual, except she just dressed in leggings and her hoodie. She made sure all her press-on nails were perfect, one of each colour, just as she always did. Then she switched it up: she put sunny yellow nail polish on all ten.

"This colour here, it's my daughter's favourite," she had said.

Kayla stayed with Little Zoe as she waited. Little Zoe smoked a lot that morning, but was determined not to use. As she hung outside Hearthstone, her hands never stopped shaking. She was going to meet her daughter and her foster mother at City Pizza. They would have pizza, then go to the park, play on the swings, climb on the Ogopogo statue.

"I'm going to try and get her back someday," Little Zoe had vowed. "I'm going to get clean again and get her back. Get both my daughters back."

And she had gotten clean for this very reason once before. It was hard for folks to get clean because rehab programs had such long wait times; she would be ready and committed to enter but then have to wait. And while waiting, she'd use, and become less ready again. But she had done it once before, had gotten into rehab, gotten clean. Last year, for six whole months.

But being clean and getting her own apartment had not seemed to make a difference—not to the Ministry. She was still denied custody, granted only supervised weekend visits. And these weekend visits were almost more painful than not seeing her daughter at all. They were a glimpse of how much she was missing, of the life going on without her.

"I did everything I could," she had said that night on Dilworth. "And it wasn't enough."

Right after that first visit, she went back into the alley where she'd smoked heroin and shot up so many times. And she used and she used, as if making up for lost time, as if for all the future times she was going to lose. Kayla hadn't been in town yet at that point. She'd only heard, later, that things had been bad. Even by street standards, things had been bad. Little Zoe had lost the apartment, lost the visits.

But she was doing better these days. Using less. Everyone could see. Not perfect, but better. She had the visits back. And, a week after that night on Dilworth Mountain, she was going to see her daughter again. At the pizza place. And then they would go to the park.

So Kayla had waited with her as she stood around smoking that morning, waiting for time to pass, trying not to pick her sunny nails. When it was time, Kayla walked with her to City Pizza.

Through the window, they could see a little girl and a woman at one of the laminate tables. The little girl had pigtails and red rubber boots, a crayon in her hand. Her face was down towards the page in front of her. Her tongue was slightly out at the side, concentrating as she coloured. The woman she was with was looking down at her artwork, a slight smile on her face. When the girl looked up, she smiled back at the woman. Smiled and then laughed at something the woman said. She still had all her baby teeth.

There was something in her eyes, something in her smile. It was the ease, the familiar comfort, the ordinariness of that smile that must have done it, the way she seemed to know there would always be a smile back. She didn't look out the window and see her mother and wave. She didn't look out and see her mother and look away. She didn't look out at all. She just smiled, so easily, and went back to colouring. Soon her tongue was out once more, her little hand moving back and forth across the page. Kayla watched her friend watch.

And then Little Zoe turned and continued down Leon, wet eyes straight ahead. Kayla followed her and watched her go down that street and into the mouth of the alley where she had gone so many times before.

That was the night Little Zoe wanted Nelson to pull the tooth.

When he did, after a haul from his bottle to steady his hands, Kayla's eyes were not on Nelson's fingers or what was happening in Little Zoe's mouth, but on her friend's eyes as her tooth was pulled. There she saw a pain so deep that it needed something physical to try and match it, but there was no matching it.

He pulled and he pulled. She never blinked.

When the tooth didn't work, there was the alley. That was where they found her.

Naomi and Marcel had been the ones to see her first, slumped against the cement wall. They had seen it before, with others, and knew what to do. Naomi, like many on the street, carried a Naloxone kit strapped to her belt loop with a carabiner. Her expert hands readied the needle quickly, and she stabbed Little Zoe in the thigh.

Naomi was a legend on the streets. She had saved people sixty-four times.

Little Zoe was already fluttering back to life when the ambulance arrived. That was when Kayla got there, summoned by the commotion, the gathering crowd.

Then her friend was on the gurney, oxygen mask on.

"She was dead for minutes," Naomi said.

"Thought she was gone for real this time," added Mama B.

Kayla would never be sure, but as the paramedics rolled the gurney away, she saw in Little Zoe's eyes a look: not of gratitude, but of anger.

Monday, 6:30 a.m.

Morning sun streamed through the beams of the half-built house where Kayla lay. She had slept well, not needing the alertness sleeping on the street demanded, and there was a hint of unexpected warmth in the air. She gathered her sleeping bag around her face and watched the day begin.

Sunrise had been Kayla's favourite time of day ever since working with the horses. On those early mornings, she had been the first person in the barn as she stepped out from her apartment beside the feed room. There was always a chorus of whinnies when the horses saw her bringing their morning hay. She loved those mornings, before anyone else arrived and the day got busy, when the time belonged just to her and the horses.

Demi Ray, the trainer, would show up at the barn next, with her three Chihuahuas trotting beside her. She walked with the self assurance of someone who had earned her own skin. She was known for bringing out the best in the horses, and also for not putting up with shit from people. She took Banamine from the vet supplies when she was hurt, and had made up for her lack of dental insurance by taking a farrier's rasp and filing her own tooth down when she had chipped it in a fall.

Sebastian would be next to arrive. He had been the crush of all the girls who hung around the stable until his desire for men became too obvious to ignore. All their tight-shirted sitting trot sessions had been for naught. Once, when he had brought a riding coach in for a lesson—a man twice his age and known for his appreciation both of good horses and young men—Kayla had heard noises coming from the hayloft. She heard a muted gasp, as if someone was in sudden pain, and instinctively grabbed a nearby pitchfork, before hearing it again and realizing that it was pleasure.

Eventually, those who boarded their horses at the farm would trickle in. Some went straight to their horses, some to Kayla with a complaint or need. Some were capable, friendly, respectful; others were more work than the horses.

When the day was done, Kayla would clean the saddles and bridles alongside Demi Ray and Sebastian. Demi Ray would tell stories. She'd been around the horse industry plenty, and had tales of helping cowboys back a truck and loaded horse trailer down a mountain, or riding a young horse, not even green broke, for the very first time.

Kayla had a story too, but she didn't know if she should tell it. It was about the contest.

Kayla had heard about the contest from Carl, before he got fired. Carl had overheard her talking to the other girls, saying how she needed to make money to buy Buddy. And Carl knew of a way to make five hundred dollars, quick. All you had to do was stay on the mechanical bull the longest. It was a bikini bull riding contest at the country-and-western bar in town.

"I know someone who would let you in, turn their eye about your age," Carl assured her.

The place was filled with guys in plaid shirts, girls in cut-off shorts and cowboy boots, leathery women in tight jeans. People on the dance floor were doing two-step. The crowd smelled of aftershave and beer.

To enter the contest, Kayla had to fill out a form. As Carl instructed, she lied about both her name and age. He told the guy at the front he knew her. Not to worry about her ID. Slipped him a twenty.

Kayla was more scared of the people than the mechanical bull. She changed in the washroom, blushing when she came out of the stall in her bikini and paddock boots. She'd borrowed the bikini from one of the other Barn Junkies, and filled it out well.

Everyone cheered as she got on. She heard those voices, took in that smell of beer. She saw Carl's excited face as he raised his bottle, toasting her. His eyes, fixed on hers, looked as if he believed in her.

She felt other eyes burning but didn't look at anyone else. Just as she did at the barn, she focused only on the ride. The mechanical bull began to buck and twist. Staying on was hard—the bull started off gentle yet pitched more furiously as it spun—but she stayed on and on and on, thinking of the money she could put towards Buddy.

When she won, Carl slapped her on the back. "That's my girl!"

She was presented with a golden trophy of a cowboy on a bucking bronco. She would keep it in her apartment: the one thing, other than her paddock boots and the photographs of her dad and grandma, that she was proud to own. She would keep the five hundred dollars there too—not enough to buy Buddy yet, but a start.

When one of the men in the bar came up to her, after, with two beers and a knowing smile, Carl stepped in front of him, glaring and bottle raised.

"Get dressed. Let's go."

The contest happened every week. But when she showed up the week after winning, bikini in her bag, the security guy at the door looked at her harder this time and said he'd need to see her ID. Carl pulled her away. She cried as he drove her back.

Carl was fired the next week. He had left the gate open, let the horses run on the golf course across the road. This was after he had driven the tractor into the side of the barn. Kayla knew his drinking had been getting worse ever since his dad had been killed in a hay baler. She couldn't get that out of her mind. She knew how balers worked.

The day Carl was gone, Patricia asked her if she wanted the job and the apartment, the one with the bucket of vomit that smelled like whiskey, the feed catalogue, and, as Kayla found later, stuffed under the mattress, half a photograph of a girl, satin piping on her plaid western shirt. On her shoulder a woman's hand. The rest of picture had been torn away.

She also found an envelope with her name on it, *Kayla,* in shaky handwriting, and $190.08 cash. *This is for Buddy*, read a ripped-off page from the feed catalogue. *I told Patricia to give you a job.*

She never saw Carl again.

But as Demi Ray told stories, she felt that the bull-riding story was one she needed other people to hear. That it was a story she had to tell.

"I..." she started one time while she, Demi Ray, and Sebastian were cleaning bridles, and there was a pause in the talk. "I..."

She was proud of the bull riding but didn't know how to tell the bikini part. And she was never good with sentences that started with "I".

Stories or not, Demi Ray liked Kayla, said she was a hard worker and respected that. And perhaps that was what she saw in Kayla—a certain sort of perseverance—when she saw her working with a young horse one day after all the chores were done. Kayla was struggling. Demi Ray told her something to try, and it worked. She gave Kayla another hint, and it worked some more. And so began the pieces of advice, the little offerings those many evenings. Demi Ray was generous with all she knew. Kayla felt her knowledge and confidence building. She worked away, night after night, riding until it was time for night check, and then watching training videos in her bed. Could this become her life, her future?

One evening, just like many evenings, Kayla tacked up one of the new horses. She was a chestnut with whites at the side of her eyes. It was March, and everything was melting, though it was too muddy in the outdoor ring to ride outside. The indoor arena it was. All was going well with the ride; the mare was a fast learner. But, as they were cantering, there was a loud sound from above. Snow was melting and sliding off the slanted roof of the arena.

The deafening rush of sound sent the mare bolting. She ripped across the arena, bucking as if auditioning for the rodeo. Kayla stayed on through it all, until the horse ran towards the wall and then turned abruptly, out from under Kayla, so impossibly fast.

There is a way to fall off a horse, to land soft: just relax and let it happen. But Kayla was determined to stay on, and her body must have been rigid, bracing as she fell. When she landed, electric pain shot through her leg, her whole body. And she heard the crack. She would never forget that sound—the sound of everything she had found for herself—made for herself—changing.

Monday, 9:00 a.m.

Where are you?

Kayla looked at the message she had sent the night before, unanswered.

You back yet? she texted Little Zoe again, hands cold in the early morning air. The sun had risen above the mountains. From where she sat in the half-built house, sleeping bag pulled around herself, she looked out at the city as it awakened.

I spent the night up in this fancy neighbourhood. A movie even got filmed here. And haha, I have a story to tell you. Made a fortune last night. If u r busy making a fortune too, maybe we can finally afford first and last months rent! :D

They had talked about getting a place before. Maybe Little Zoe could use her ID to secure a room. They could pool their money for the deposit. Little Zoe spent her money as soon as she earned it, but perhaps things could be different this time.

So text me, ok? I'm worried. But she wanted to keep it casual, if only to reassure herself. *Yeah, I have stories from last night. You'd be proud.*

They told each other stories of their days and nights. Whether they spoke of a date they could have done without or something that made them laugh—there was plenty—they were there for each other and confirmed it in the telling of their words.

Little Zoe knew about Kayla's childhood and how the stables had been her sanctuary, just as Kayla knew about the foster homes in which Little Zoe had grown up, the many times she had run away until she was gone for good. Before the street, running was her only constant. She was used to moving on from specks of towns, moving on from pull-out arcs beside highways, moving on from people who hurt her and people who she thought might. And then there were the people she had hurt—and there were those too, she said, much as she never meant to.

They had shared stories of the past, as if tip-toeing into the lake. Just not everything.

But just as Kayla had told Little Zoe she'd be a natural rider—*Your hips know what they're doing*—she had told Little Zoe about the bull-riding contest and how she earned her trophy.

"Damn girl!" Little Zoe had said when Kayla told her. "You've got it in you!"

Kayla wished she could still feel her hug.

She noticed a man on the road up ahead, taking his dog for a morning walk. After watching the sunrise, she had fallen back asleep, groggy with the luxury of time away from the street. Seeing the man, she was instantly awake. She knew the dangers of sleeping where you weren't supposed to be. Getting caught in a nice neighbourhood like this, trespassing in someone else's half-built house, wasn't good. She peeled out of her sleeping bag and started pulling on her boots. Perhaps she could be on the sidewalk before he noticed her.

But it was too late. He waved. His dog started wagging.

"Morning," he called, as if trying to make the best of an awkward situation.

"Morning."

The dog trotted over to her on his extendable leash. He had one brown eye and one blue.

"Supposed to warm up today," the man said jovially. "Spring is finally on its way."

So he was going to pretend everything was normal?

"Great. I'd really welcome spring," Kayla offered. She decided to play along and pet the dog.

"The trades will be by soon," the man continued with a hint of caution. "Working on this house. They come pretty early. Just so you know."

She continued rolling her sleeping bag as he continued on his way. She was hoisting her pack onto her back when a woman pushing an empty baby stroller appeared at the curve of the road.

"Kayla."

Kayla stopped. What the hell?

"It's Livia, from outreach." Livia looked the same as she did those nights: slightly mussed. Her hair was pulled into a messy ponytail and her scarf had come undone. And then there was the empty stroller.

"Hi."

"I just dropped my daughter off at preschool." She looked down the hill from where she had come. "I…I was just thinking of Zoe, actually…"

"I still don't know where she is. She's not answering my messages."

Livia nodded slowly. "Wanjiru and I filed a police report."

"The cops say anything?"

"They took the information you gave us. Said they would look into it." She paused. "But…what are you doing right now? Want something to eat? I live near here."

The idea of somewhere warm and some food was appealing. "You don't have to."

"I'd like to." Livia smiled. "It's not far."

They headed down the street towards where the houses were fully built, the trees taller than newly planted sticks. They went past Valentine's lawn decorations and fountains in front yards, a woman in yoga pants walking her dog. Finally, Livia stopped in front of a two-storey house with a Christmas wreath still on the door.

The warmth hit Kayla as soon as she stepped inside. She took it all in.

Ceilings stretched up two stories in the back of a large open-concept room. There were lots of big windows, but the blinds were drawn. Nice furniture decorated the place, along with plates of encrusted food and empty glasses. Framed photographs—of Livia and a man and a little girl, of mountains, and of what could have been a sunrise or sunset—adorned the walls. Children's books and toys were strewn on the carpet, along with a half-built house of Lego surrounded by pieces. The place smelled vaguely of wine—or perhaps that was Livia's breath.

"Welcome," Livia said, taking off her coat.

Kayla put down her pack and took off her shoes. It wasn't quite like being in a client's house. She wasn't sure what to do.

"Come on in. Can I get you a coffee or anything? Something to eat?"

Livia took a canvas bag out of the bottom of the stroller. Bottles clinked. She brought the clinking bag through the kitchen and then disappeared into a well-stocked pantry, only part of which Kayla could see. So much food. Then she came out to the kitchen.

"Coffee's made. Just have to heat it up." She set cups on the counter. Her hands were shaking. "It's nice to have you over. I've always wanted to get to know you better."

Kayla wasn't sure what to say. "I really appreciate that coat and sleeping bag you gave me. And Little Zoe loves her unicorn necklace."

"I'm glad she likes it. I just wish we'd hear from her."

"Me too."

Livia made the coffees, took hers into the pantry. Kayla heard the sound of something pouring quietly.

"Want me to make you pancakes? Or I have leftover pizza if you'd prefer."

"I'd love some pizza."

Livia put two slices of pizza on a plate and began microwaving. "So...you stayed up here for the night then?"

"I had a date and was tired."

"It's funny, actually," Livia laughed. "We stayed in each other's places last night. I was downtown looking for Little Zoe after outreach. Got too tired to drive, so spent the night in my car. And you...seems you spent the night in the house we're building."

"That's your house? Sorry for sleeping in it." Oh. That said, if she were going to squat in anyone's house, at least she happened to choose the house of an outreach volunteer who would hopefully understand. But something in Livia's eyes, and perhaps on her breath, this hour of the morning, made Kayla sorry for her in other ways. "The house is going to be really nice. Great view."

Livia handed Kayla the plate of steaming pizza. "Thanks," she said. "We need a change."

There was something about those words that reminded Kayla of her mother. After Kayla's dad and grandma died, but before Kayla's mother started moving in with boyfriends, they had constantly switched apartments and trailer homes, her mother always saying she needed a change. As though her unhappiness was the dwelling's fault.

Kayla could remember how envious she had been of her neighbour in one of those early places, a ramshackle bungalow they lived in before Silvercreek. He was a boy her own age who lived in the bigger house next door, and he had planted a tree with his parents in their backyard. His parents called it his tree and said it would grow as he grew, and would always be there. Kayla remembered yearning for that feeling of permanence, for something to call her own, something she could help grow. So she had planted a chestnut that fell from a tree at school. It was a shiny brown chestnut and, in the scrap of grass behind trailer they rented, she planted it, watered the bare dirt, and waited for it to grow. But of course they left that place, just as they left all places, before anything could emerge from the ground.

Not long after that, they'd moved into Silvercreek Gardens. Where there was no garden. Where That One came long. Where he didn't wait for her to grow.

And she had endured, waiting for the words to tell her mother, waiting for the words to even come to herself.

But one day he was just gone, her mother cleaning the house furiously, saying, *That motherfucker is out of here.* So was the brown and orange plaid couch. That was the day after Kayla's mother said, *Next time you get a nosebleed on the furniture you tell me,* and all Kayla had said was, *I didn't get a nosebleed.*

Monday, 10:00 a.m.

"So any leads on Little Zoe?" Livia asked, snapping Kayla back into the present. Memories had a way of holding her, sometimes in ways she didn't want. Time was a one-way line, Cerise had once said, high, and Kayla remembered that because for her it felt different: experience, for her, was more like a collage of pictures, overlapping and moving, details not always clear, but some standing out so intensely they burned more brightly than the rest.

"No," Kayla told her. "But that might not mean anything. She's probably just on an extended date and lost her phone. Or maybe someone whisked her away on vacation."

Such things were possible, escorting. Maybe someone had brought her to a foreign country where she didn't have a SIM card. They'd all heard of such things happening. Did Little Zoe have a passport? They knew the phrase from some escorting ads: must be passport ready.

Kayla conjured an image of Little Zoe lying on a beach somewhere, tropical drink in hand, a pasty old man on a lounge chair beside her. Kayla wasn't naïve enough to fantasize otherwise, but she blocked the image of him from her mind, preferring to envision just Little Zoe, soaking up the sun as she loved to do. Little Zoe would make the most of wherever she went.

"Or maybe she finally got into rehab," Kayla found herself saying, thinking of possibilities. "She said she'd go the minute they let her in. Maybe it's one of those programs where they take away your phone."

"I'd be happy if any of that were the case," Livia said. "But at least the police know now. And we did an alert for the other outreach volunteers. Everyone will be looking for her."

"We all are too." Her friends were used to people coming and going though. Kayla felt oddly alone in her panic. But she also knew Little Zoe best.

"Or she could be in jail," Kayla realized. "If she got arrested, she wouldn't be able to contact us. And maybe...maybe she doesn't want to contact us. Sometimes she talked about just leaving the street. Starting fresh. Sometimes she wished she could just pick up and leave this life. Because it was the only way. But I thought she'd..."

"Did she have any family she could go back to?"

Wasn't she family? But as for other family, Little Zoe had aged out of the foster care system. She had never been in one place for long. Perhaps one reason why Little Zoe made friends so easily was because she always had to do so fast. That was another reason why she could be so many places now. She was an expert in how to quickly make and remake herself.

"No, Little Zoe didn't have anyone to go back to," Kayla answered. The family she had was her chosen family on the street. And that was why it was so hard for Kayla to believe she would have left without a word.

"What about you? You have family...elsewhere?"

When Kayla was living at the barn, she had visited her mother for exactly one day. She thought things might have been different, that she had remembered wrong, judged too much. But while she was at her mother's, her mother just fawned over a different rent-paying boyfriend, asked questions like she barely knew her, smiled a lot, and offered Kayla a drink. One visit was enough.

"I had my grandma." Just saying her grandma's name, she was flooded with the scent of tomatoes from the garden and the taste of her chocolate chip cookies. She remembered how her grandma would say she was taking dolls to the doll hospital whenever they got ripped, bending over the sewing machine and giving operating room reports. They were always going to be fine.

"But I don't have a childhood home to go back to." Then she thought of her real home: the barn.

"I'm sorry." Livia seemed uncertain what to say. She paused, shifted. "Wanjiru thinks we should make some posters. You have a photo of Little Zoe?"

Kayla shook her head. "Lily might. She's always taking pics on her phone."

"Lily's the one with the infected arm, right?"

"Yeah." The one who loved soccer and tried to get folks to play in the park. The one who was generous with her sushi or curry when she had any. The one with the beautiful singing voice.

"I'll keep looking for Little Zoe," Livia continued, then noticed Kayla's empty plate. "You want more to eat? Help yourself."

"Yeah. Thanks." Kayla rose to go to the fridge. Taped there was a picture in crayon drawn by a child's hand; it was of a girl on what might have been a trike. Her eyes were two circles, and on her face was a crooked smile. A figure was behind her, with a beard. Careful handwriting spelled out DAD. There was no mom in the picture.

Livia was looking at her. "So, I've always wondered...couldn't help but notice...you have a limp?"

"I do. I've got metal from my hip to my knee. I had a riding accident. I used to ride horses. But the doctors said I would never ride again. But it's alright. I'm fine now."

"Fine," Livia repeated, as if trying the word out in her mouth. Then she looked at Kayla harder. "I know about being fine. What happened?"

Monday, 10:30 a.m.

Kayla hadn't told Little Zoe and Cerise much about her life with horses. When she'd started to explain one night at their corner, Cerise made it clear—*That's for rich bitches.* Kayla hadn't mentioned horses again. What she'd experienced was too sacred to risk being contaminated with misunderstanding and judgment. It wasn't just about riding; it was about being around horses, in their presence. Being.

Sitting here, at a kitchen table in a fancy house with Livia, who was sweet but basically a stranger, she didn't know how she could possibly explain what horses meant to her. But she could at least tell her about the accident.

After her fall, she'd needed surgery, hospitalization. She was given a regimen of drugs that would have thrilled some of her new friends on Leon, like Lily, who had once been a high school soccer star, but got addicted to painkillers after surgery for a torn ACL. Kayla's pain had been intense, but not as bad as the realization that she'd never be able to ride again. She took the pills both to relieve the physical pain and to keep from thinking about what she'd lost.

The surgeon had never seen a fracture so bad in someone Kayla's age. She would need a walker at first, but with a few months of diligent exercises she would be able to walk with crutches. Then a cane. But probably always with a limp.

Demi Ray picked her up from the hospital and settled her back in at the farm. Patricia and John let her stay for free, even though she couldn't work, because she didn't cost them anything. The woman they hired to replace her didn't want to live in the barn.

Demi Ray tucked Kayla into bed with a gentleness that was surprising, given the efficiency of her hands in the barn. She made sure Kayla had her pills and a glass of water by her bed. Although Demi Ray's culinary skills consisted of pressing buttons on a microwave and opening cans, she brought takeout pizza and protein bars and yogurt, and she put threatening notes in the tack room fridge for others not to eat the food. Sebastian, who had started bringing his first real boyfriend to the barn, baked her brownies. The women who boarded their horses at the stable pitched in and got her flowers and a card.

Demi Ray would let herself into Kayla's apartment at the end of every day. She would tell her how the horses were coming along. Kayla listened numbly. Sebastian brought her old copies of *Practical Horseman* magazine. She thanked him but wouldn't have picked them up even if her mind had been made for reading. She wasn't ready to think of what she might never do again.

Demi Ray saw the untouched magazines, the empty pill bottle beside her bed. "You're still watching training videos, right? You're not the type to give up."

Every day, Kayla shuffled back and forth to the washroom, the walker scraping the floor. She did her rehabilitation exercises in front of Buddy's stall so she would have company.

Every day, Demi Ray would come by, taking off her winter boots, which leaked so much she wore plastic bags inside. When spring warmed towards summer, she brought with her the scent of outside into the stale apartment, reminding Kayla of those afternoons when they would take the truck to the feed store, windows down and music up, wind rushing at their faces, the smell of fresh-cut hay in the air.

Every day, Kayla listened as water dripped from the rooftop, voices came and voices left. She heard the new stable hand feed the horses every morning, watched the patterns of the sun as it made its way through her tiny window and across the ceiling. Shadows came, disappeared, came again.

One day, Demi Ray's walk was slightly different. Kayla could tell before she spoke that something had changed.

"I'm moving to Florida," she said. "I've been hired to ride a great mare down there. She's almost at Grand Prix. They want me to help get her to that level."

Florida was where the biggest horse shows were held every winter, where the top horses competed, where a rider could make a name for themselves. Demi Ray had been offered a chance there once before, on a horse that she had trained from the basics. But when he became valuable the owner had him sold out from under her. It was the only time Kayla had seen her cry.

"They won't sell her on you?"

"They liked how I rode her so much they said they'd sign a contract. And she really is a wonderful mare."

"A great mare will fight with you, but in the end, will always fight for you." They said it at the same time. Just one of the quotes that Demi Ray had taught her.

"When do you leave?"

"Next week."

Demi Ray wasn't one for hugging, nor for long goodbyes. The day she packed her tack trunk into her pickup truck, she took a picture on Kayla's phone: Kayla standing beside Buddy, without her walker. Buddy's head was turned toward her. Their eyes were on each other rather than the camera. Kayla printed that photograph and kept it, along with the ones of her dad and her grandma, tucked away in the deep heart of her backpack.

Kayla listened to the closing of Demi Ray's truck door, watched the truck's taillights grow smaller and smaller down the road. She stared at the dust as it fell slowly back to the ground.

Kayla's life became even quieter after that, mostly just the sounds she heard through her walls. Sebastian brought her gossip and pizza at least once a week, but he was her only company. Every day she walked a bit further, graduating to crutches, and then to just one crutch. She would brush Buddy in his stall, taking care not to put weight on her bad leg, talking to him in low tones. But it pained her to see him ridden by others, especially after it was clear that he was sore in the back. She stayed in her room when he was ridden in lessons.

She stayed in her room a lot. There was nowhere for her to go, with her body or with her mind. The accident had scarred more than her leg, broken more than just her bones. She slept often and deep. The pills helped her drift through the days.

Early one morning, as if in the fragments of a dream, she heard a familiar clomp of hooves. Buddy's. The familiarity was enough to wake her, but then there were only distant sounds from outside, the stirring of the horses, the scurrying of mice. She drifted.

Later, when she left her apartment to brush Buddy, she saw his stall was empty. She limped to where the stable hand was pulling the wheelbarrow into the barn.

"Where's Buddy?"

The stable hand turned from where she stood, pitchfork in hand. She wouldn't look at Kayla.

"Left this morning. Sold to a buyer out of town."

Monday, Noon

"I'm so sorry about Buddy," Livia said. They had moved from the kitchen table to the couch in the living room, where two-storey windows looked onto the backyard. The sun was high. Icicles dripped from the eaves. "Do you have a picture of him?"

Kayla retrieved the picture from her backpack: a love-shiny, scarred horse, beautiful to her if not to others. Beside him stood a different version of herself, one who was provinces and a world away. Not even a year ago.

"There's a lot of love in that picture," Livia mused, reaching out but then stopping, as if sensing the memory was Kayla's to hold.

"There's lots of love in your pictures, too," Kayla said, suddenly wanting to change the subject. She looked from her own photograph to the framed portrait of Livia with a man and a little girl. Their faces were smiling, but Livia had a pained determination in her eyes, the man a stiffness.

"That's my husband, Tom, and my daughter, Cara. She's four now. That was last Christmas."

"Beautiful family."

"They are." But there was a tinge of sadness to her voice, and she disappeared into the pantry again with her cup. She returned with a mostly full mug, topped it up with coffee and sugar.

Through the window, Kayla could see a couple of people were walking their dogs, coats open. From down the street came the shudder of a backboard after a basketball hit it, voices cheering, the sounds of teenagers having a lunch-hour pick-up game. Along the sidewalk, a dog was running alongside a young girl on a skateboard.

"This is the sort of day to bring people out of hibernation," Livia mused.

The people who have a choice to hibernate, Kayla couldn't help but think.

"I've been hibernating a bit," Livia admitted with a shrug and a sip. "So many days I just stay in bed all day and can't move. Outreach gets me out of the house. Because I want to help someone. I really do. Someone who can be helped. But some days I just stay in bed..."

A bed to stay in. Not like Old Nelson, not like Eddie, not like a lot of them, who had to deal with what they had to deal with without the comfort of a bed.

But then Kayla saw Livia's body start to shake with sobs.

"Half the time I don't even know what day it is. I just know it's a weekday because I hear Tom getting Cara ready for preschool. Sometimes I hear myself talking, wishing them a good day, and I don't know if it's me. It's like I don't know what 'me' is any more. Or if there's anyone inside at all. Sometimes I just lie in bed and watch the shadows slide across the ceiling as the day goes by. That's how I know time happened, that I through another day. *Got through*—listen to me. How can I talk of my life that way?"

She stood up. "Fuck it. Mind if I have a glass of wine? It's after noon. Five o'clock somewhere. Dark under the porch. All that."

She did, then came back, wiping her eyes.

"Sorry. It's been...a while. But it's like there's a deadness inside me. It's...how I see things. Or don't see them anymore. So... I do whatever it takes to feel different..."

She stared out the window.

"I used to like taking pictures. That used to be a way of celebrating something beautiful...it was a way of seeing, a way of trying to explore something that's beyond the surface...I used to remember feeling so fascinated...But I haven't taken pictures in a long time. Can't even pick up my camera. It's like I can't see the world the way I used to. Like the beauty is gone."

Kayla felt a stab of recognition. She knew how it felt to have beauty be gone.

"After I had Cara, I was so exhausted. Felt this odd mix of inexplicable sadness and terror. I didn't know what was real any more. I kept thinking: how can I feel this way? When this is what I wanted, when this was what made me so happy? But the darkness...that terrifying emptiness...how could it be both? But it was. And it wasn't something I could shake off or separate from myself because it was me. How I saw the world. How I was in the world—or wasn't in the world. Did I put so much energy into making someone else that...?"

She put her head in her hands.

Kayla looked at her, letting her know it was alright to continue. She knew about stories that were hard to tell, and the importance of the telling, however it came.

"I stopped taking pictures because I didn't know what was real any more. I didn't trust the way I saw the world."

She reached for a tissue.

"Tom took Cara for long walks. He'd call me from work, a few times a day. He always sounded relieved when I answered. And wine became my way to cope. Something to help me relax. Get through the day. At first it was just a drink before dinner. Then as early as I could. I would set Cara up on the baby mat with her toys and then pour myself a glass. Then two. Then three. And I tried pills. I went to the doctor, begging to feel better. Eventually we found a medication, but with the meds came a numbness. I lost the brightness I'd once known, any spark. They let me function. I could go through the motions of daily life. But where did *I* go?"

She took another sip.

"It was as if everything was on low on those meds. But from the outside I was doing better. I no longer had that look in my eye that made people wary. And I tried to hide the emptiness. To do the things. I tried to take Cara to story times, the park. And I was grateful to know what was real, and to be what everyone said was getting better. I kept holding onto that. And I had this beautiful family—so much to be happy about. I would go to playgroup circles, do the nursery rhymes. I'd sing, 'Hop Hop Little Bunnies'. I'd come home. Try to be fine. Wine helped. Let me relax a bit. It was like I was trying for something to be beautiful again. See glimmers of something better. So I chased and chased it. Except then it became always one step ahead, one more sip away..."

She smiled sadly.

"I tried to hide it. Once Tom went to work, I'd put Cara in the stroller, surrounded by toys and board books. Like a good mother. Before opening time, I'd line up alongside others outside the liquor store. People just like me. I'd wait along with the guy in the business suit who smelled like aftershave—on his breath, too—and the woman in Lululemon yoga pants. She would lean against the brick of the wall as soon as she got outside, both hands around her can of cider so anyone walking by couldn't see what was inside. Lean back and drink until her hands stopped shaking. But I would wait to drink until I got home. I'd set Cara down with her toys, make sure she was content, pull the blinds. Sometimes, pouring that first glass, my own hands shook."

Her hands were shaking less as she was telling the story.

"Before Tom got home, I'd double wrap the bottles in plastic bags and put them in the diaper bag in the bottom of the stroller. Take Cara to the park and throw them out when no one was looking. I kept working. I was functional. Careful. And I went back to taking pictures, but just with my phone. I couldn't make art any more. I had to put that terrifying world of not knowing what was real behind me. Taking pictures felt too frightening to risk. And I drank. Hoping to feel something else, something closer to good. But what I long for...what I long for is that beautiful feeling I used to feel..."

She let out a long sigh. Kayla just nodded, ever so slightly.

"But enough about me. I'm rambling. What I really want to do is help find Little Zoe."

"I want to find her too. And you're not rambling. You're hurting. Pain is not a pissing contest. Just because I've had things rough doesn't mean I can't be there for someone else. It means I can be. Because I know how much that matters."

She felt more words on their way.

"And I know about the beauty being gone. I know what it's like not to do what you love anymore. What it's like not to see the world the way you once could."

That was why she had needed to leave, that night back in August. To preserve what had been beautiful. To at least keep that.

Before: The End

She had left the farm on a night when the frogs and crickets were so loud they were screaming. Hobbling up the long driveway from the barn to the road, she just listened to them. They were the only sounds after the stirrings of horses in their stalls, the sound of her own footsteps through the barn, that door closing behind her.

That night she left the single crutch behind: she felt ready to walk on her own, and the time to leave was now. She grabbed her backpack, the slim pile of cash she'd saved, and a clean shirt. And the photographs of her dad, grandma, and Buddy. There had been no time to pack anything else.

She washed her hands and face in the culvert down the road, once she was off the property, listening for any footsteps following her, the starting of the truck. She scrubbed furiously, rinsed her mouth with the brackish water.

Then she walked towards the gas station, along the side of the road, ready to sink into the deep grasses in the ditch if a certain truck came by. But surely he couldn't drive after...

A vehicle did approach. She had heard it in the distance, coming up behind her. She ducked into the bushes at the side of the road, breathing fast. A pickup truck came into view, but it wasn't the truck she feared. She threw up in the bushes, her whole body shaking. She could not get enough out.

With hands that had to be calm, she changed into the fresh shirt. She took the bloody shirt she had been wearing, wrapped it in a rock, and sank it into the dark water of the culvert.

The walk to the gas station was long and painful for her bad hip and leg, but she got there somehow. When she asked the attendant for the washroom key, she could feel him looking, but he handed it over. Under the fluorescent glare of the washroom, she scrubbed her face and hands, then rinsed her hair until the tips were only violet again. She watched the blood spiral down the drain.

She looked at herself in the mirror, regretting not what she had done, but only that she'd had to do it. And she had.

She had.

*

Back in her tiny apartment, beside the feed room, there was a man on the floor, still breathing.

He was a man she had seen for years but hardly knew. She remembered him most for how he drove the tractor, the way he watched the girls in their riding lessons, his hazel eyes, and his walk—those slow, easy footsteps, assured, as if to remind everyone that he owned the farm and everything in it.

He had let himself into her apartment while she was sleeping. There was no lock on the door for the hired help. The sound of the door, that small click, was hardly enough to wake her, given the pills. She only stirred in that way sleepers do when they have learned never to trust.

His hand was over her mouth. Then his other hand was pulling at her clothing.

She screamed a suffocated scream, but Patricia was away for the weekend at a horse auction, and there were no other houses nearby.

She realized she didn't want to bite his hand. No. What she did bite, when the time came, was what she had taken into her mouth as he stood before her. Her on her knees, his hand on the back of her head.

And she bit.

She bit for that moment and for all the moments that had come before, for the girl who had felt the scratch of a brown and orange plaid couch, for the girl who had learned not to raise her voice and had hidden her words in the neck of a horse. She bit for all those times she had not bitten.

And she bit hard.

Before: Leaving

She watched him as he slumped to the floor, passing out with the pain, moaning but breathing. And bleeding. There was so much blood. She had to leave, and leave fast.

Perhaps she could have claimed self defense, and perhaps they would have believed her. Perhaps. She could have stayed, gone through it all. But what if they charged her with assault? What if he had bled out and died? What then?

She kept checking the online newspaper of her hometown, checking as she travelled across the country and well after, but there had been no news. So he must have been alright. Alive at least. But she felt compelled to stay away and keep her head low. And nothing was left for her there anyway. She only had her memories of the farm, of the place she loved so deeply, and she wanted to keep them intact. She needed to keep something.

So she had left, her feet going up the driveway, leaving the one place she ever felt was home.

Monday, 2:00 p.m.

But Kayla told Livia none of this. She just stared out the window, watching sunlight catch on the icicles as they melted, admiring that ability to transform.

"I need to pick up Cara from preschool soon," Livia said, putting her wine glass on the counter. Then she got a clean coffee mug and poured a fresh cup. She didn't go into the pantry. "But maybe we could go on a walk first. Get some fresh air. I'll take you to the creek. It's a place I like to go."

Kayla snapped herself back into the present.

"A walk would be great." Kayla followed Livia to the foyer. As they were putting on their coats, Livia's phone buzzed. She ducked into the living room to take it, was back in a moment. "That was Wanjiru. She's going to come by for dinner. We'll all cook together."

Kayla liked the sound of that. She put on her coat and followed Livia out the door.

The creek wasn't far. It was past where Livia's new house was being built, through thickets of bushes that were just bare sticks this time of year. A narrow deer path wound through them. Last year's reeds and grasses were long and brown, laid flat by snow that had since melted. Where the creek ran down the hillside—mostly frozen, with only a trickle of running water—bubbles were trapped beneath the ice.

"I liked to take pictures here," Livia began. "The way the light reflects, the way the creek flows. Other seasons, there's a real rush of water, but...it's like I can't go back to that..."

Kayla wasn't sure what to say. She wanted to be encouraging, but understood not being able to go back to what you loved. Not being able to see the world the way you once did.

Since leaving the farm, there was now a lot of ugliness in her world. Successful as times like last night's date could be, there was ugliness in the way some tricks saw her, as though she were just a collection of body parts to be used. Meat. She knew she was not *that*—she had made a promise to herself on that very first date—but sometimes it was hard to feel otherwise.

And living on the streets, there was ugliness in the way people looked at her, as if she didn't have a right to exist. There was ugliness in the way people wouldn't look at her too, as they walked by her on the sidewalk, as though she were invisible. It was hard for that not to become the way she saw herself.

Yet Little Zoe had helped her see differently. She had shown Kayla it was possible to see beyond ugliness and pain, that their ghosts didn't have to haunt them. At least not in a way that kept them from living.

That there could always be something more.

So perhaps her friend had gone away to find that. *To live.*

She tried to fathom all the possibilities.

Little Zoe, she wondered, *did you found something more?*

Monday, 3:00 p.m.

"Mommy!"

The little girl with pigtails and a painting smock came running as soon as Livia and Kayla stepped inside the preschool. But Kayla saw in her eyes a look she knew well herself: one that wondered which version of her mother she would see.

"Cara, sweetie. How was your day?" A hug, a kiss on the cheek. Kayla wondered if Livia was still feeling that emptiness, or if she had found enough to sustain her to exist in this world?

"I painted a stegosaurus. His name is Wilbur."

"Wonderful! This is my friend Kayla." Livia helped Cara out of her painting smock and into her coat.

Cara looked at Kayla. "Hi. My best friend is Jaspreet. We're the queens of dinosaur land."

Walking home—Cara pushing her own stroller—the girl recounted her day of adventures, and Livia made encouraging noises, asked questions. Tried.

As they approached the house, Cara ran ahead, and Livia turned to Kayla.

"I sometimes think I should try to take pictures again. Pictures like the ones I used to take. Of how the world can be. Just on my phone. Just a start. Just to see."

*

Wanjiru came at four o'clock, carrying canvas bags of groceries. She walked in like she had been there many times before. She gave Kayla a crushing hug in that big way of hers, not asking why she was there. She went to Cara after setting the groceries on the counter, watching the girl build Lego.

"And how are you, Cara?"

"Super duper." Cara returned to building and humming a little song. Kayla could see it was true. She didn't seem to know the fragility around her. Or perhaps she went on anyway in that resilient and forgiving way of kids. For now.

"We can make some *githeri*," Wanjiru said, pulling cans of kidney beans and corn from the bag.

"Can I help?" Kayla asked.

"Of course." Wanjiru handed Kayla onions. "Chop these."

They watched as Livia poured herself a big glass of wine. "Would either of you like some?"

"No thanks," Kayla said, looking down at the onions. She found a knife and began to chop.

"Same here. But thanks." Wanjiru took a can opener from the drawer. "My *cucu*—my grandmother—taught me how to make *githeri*, when I was Cara's age." She poured the cans into a pot and began chopping tomatoes. "We ate it often. Nothing came from cans, of course." She started to recall her *cucu*—a woman fierce even by Wanjiru's standards, who sang Mau Mau freedom songs while stoking the fire, who loved her co-wife more than her husband—and Kayla thought of her own grandmother. Of how different things might have been, if only.

But there was always an *if only*. What mattered was what you did with the now.

That sounded like something Little Zoe would say.

Once dinner was over and they had all washed the dishes, Livia sat on the couch with Cara and read her a few storybooks. Her empty wineglass stayed on the counter. She kept drifting in and out of sleep after Cara started snoring gently.

"I guess our evening's wrapping up here," Wanjiru said. "You staying the night?"

"Not sure." Staying in a warm bed sounded great, but she didn't want to impose.

"You could stay with me. I have to teach an early class, but you could come with me if you want."

"You're welcome to stay here," Livia said, stirring from the couch. She rose as Wanjiru gave Kayla a hug goodbye. "I bet you'll want a shower. Let me show you the guest room. And get you some towels. And thank you, Wanjiru."

The shower felt amazing, just as it had on the farm after a long day's work, when the cold had settled into her bones. But the cold she had come to know on the streets was like no other.

She emerged from the shower, towel wrapped around her, and padded into the guest bedroom where Livia had laid out pajamas. They were flannel, with a matching top and bottom. Kayla had only seen people wear ones like them in movies.

Livia had left her bedroom door open, in case Kayla needed anything. Kayla could see her curled up with Cara on the bed. Both snored softly.

Kayla walked around the darkened house. She couldn't help but think of all the things around her, things Kori or Teflon would want to steal. Livia had never done anything but trust.

Kayla thought about how she had started the day in the half-built skeleton of Livia's new house and was now in her home, with all the good and bad it held. She spent a long time walking around, touching surfaces that only looked shiny until she got up close.

Once in bed, with a comforter as thick as the one in the storefront window downtown, Kayla closed her eyes. There was no need for half-awake listening, for detecting footsteps. There was nothing but the hum of the furnace and the strange quiet of the night, the darkness as she closed her eyes. She knew then, drifting, that this would be a sleep deep enough to dream.

Tuesday, 9:00 a.m.

You looked so peaceful, Kayla, I didn't want to wake you, read the note on Livia's kitchen table. *I'm just taking Cara to school. Help yourself to anything you want in the kitchen. Stay as long as you want. I like having you here. If you need to go, here's a few dollars to get you downtown. I hope you'll stay.*

But she had to go.

While talking with Livia and Wanjiru the night before, Kayla's excuses for Little Zoe's disappearance sounded so thin. She had hoped that Little Zoe would come back with some reason, some story. Yet when she had heard the forced assuredness in her own voice, she realized just how scared she actually was.

She had texted Cerise and Ketchum the night before but needed to check back in with Naomi, who liked to know what everyone was up to, and with Mama B, who always knew what to do.

Thank you for everything, she wrote at the bottom of the note after eating a few leftovers. *See you out there. Let's keep each other posted, if we hear anything about Little Zoe.* She crossed it out. *Anything from Little Zoe.*

Once downtown, she looked for her friends in the usual places. She hadn't charged her battery to text them but figured she would find them this way. She walked past storefronts for lease, the drop-in medical clinic with its metal grille on the window, the Friendship Society, the places that made up her neighbourhood, the places that had become her life now.

Nestled amongst the businesses was an unlikely old bungalow with an unfenced garden. Everything had been built up around it, but it remained. There were raised garden beds, vacant save for tangles of last year's growth, gnarled fruit trees. This was where she and Little Zoe had picked peaches last August, apples in September. *Help yourself,* read a small hand-painted sign, and people did. Here you could also get water on sweltering summer days. Kayla remembered seeing people coming and going from that place last summer, even folks from the street: skinny girls in tank tops bent over the gardens, getting sunburnt as they dug in the soil, guys with arms purpled with tattoos harvesting scarlet runner beans. Once there had even been a little boy with one of the women, picking carrots from the earth and holding them up to the sun. She could still see Little Zoe there too, happy with her hands in the dirt. But as she walked past, Kayla had an inexplicable feeling she wouldn't be with her there again, not quite like that. But maybe it was just the change of season. And no moment can be just like another.

She tried to shake that missing feeling as she walked on.

Over there was the beat-up camper van that had taken the working girls to Scandia once. The van's owner, a jovial hippie, was known to give the girls drugs in exchange for services, but was sometimes up for other fun too. He'd taken the girls to Scandia Golf & Games and Family Fun Centre. He had just enjoyed watching the girls enjoy, wanting nothing more in return. They had raced go-carts, tried mini golf, played arcade games, ate pizza and buttery popcorn. They spent hours playing and seeing little tickets emerge from dispensers in a room with a sign that read Redemption Games. *It's like I'm a kid again,* Cerise had said, grabbing tickets to redeem prizes, but Kayla was less focused on that; in the playing she felt a newness rather than the pain of being a child. But there was a certain childlike joy of being there too. She remembered the look on Little Zoe's face as they played: a sweetness, an openness, an innocence.

Little Zoe, I miss you. Kayla found herself talking to her friend in her head.

She approached the van. Maybe if that guy were there, she could ask him if he'd seen Little Zoe. Maybe she'd even be with him. Days and nights of fun, warm beds, free drugs. But no one was in the van. She lingered near the back, but it was quiet, too.

Kayla had to keep going.

Walking by an alley, Kayla saw a single crutch stamped with *Kelowna General Hospital.* She'd gone to that hospital once, with Lily when her arm had turned bad and she'd stopped making sense. Septic, Mama B identified. And Mama B had been out here long enough to know. Lily hadn't wanted to go, but Mama B insisted.

Kayla remembered that day. At the hospital it was hard to get your fix, so many people avoided the hospital at all costs, even if the costs were great. But they'd convinced Lily to go. Kayla had gone with her, waiting in the emergency room among old people with chest pain and toddlers howling with earaches. Kayla watched people go in before Lily, people holding their chests or stomachs, one with blood running down his face. But when the swollen ankle got called in ahead of her and came back with an ace bandage before Lily even got in, Lily had stormed through the swinging doors deeper into the hospital.

Kayla followed her, past people shuffling in hospital gowns and others lying on gurneys, nurses in their rubber-soled shoes looking at her in her high-heeled boots. Walking past one of the rooms, Kayla saw a girl from the street. She was someone Kayla hadn't known well enough to miss. An IV was strapped to her hand, with a bag of liquid hanging above. Her skin was yellow, just so yellow.

"Tell somebody I'm here," the girl had said. "Please tell somebody I'm here."

Little Zoe, Kayla felt herself saying, *could you be there?*

As if asking into the air could bring answers.

She had to walk on.

Kayla continued past the liquor store across from the city courts, where the usuals lingered, along with some underage kids calculating the best way to get drunk on the money they had. The usuals would no doubt buy something for themselves when the kids sent one of them inside.

There was the Indian restaurant that smelled so good and gave takeaway containers of food out the back door, no questions asked. Not all business owners were so kind: the owner of another restaurant had hurled dog shit at Marta when she had camped too close to his doorway.

There was the Thai place from which one of Kayla's johns had gotten takeout. He had wanted to try a girlfriend experience, he said, and actually ended up treating her like one: they ate with chopsticks in a motel, watching TV. During sex, he tried to pleasure her. After it was over, he cried, saying *I'm sorry, Jesus, I'm sorry.* He had asked her if they could pray. She had asked him if she could stay and have a bath. In the bath, she slid all the way to her neck with the water around her, felt her hair float around her face. She thought of Mama B, who always longed for a bath, but couldn't afford to rent a room herself. Someday, along with enough for first and last month's rent, Kayla would get enough to rent Mama B a room so she could enjoy at least this. At that moment she had savoured its warmth and enjoyed it for them both. That was important out here: to enjoy what you could enjoy, when you could, and to enjoy it for those you loved as well. Wishing you could share those experiences, sharing them without actually sharing them, was a strange way of caring for one another, but it had to do in this life.

Kayla continued past a tattoo parlour and the pizza place where Little Zoe had seen her daughter. Kayla felt a wash of pain for her friend. Pain—they shared that too. If she could have taken on some of her friend's pain that day, and for all the other hard days, she would have. But of course she couldn't.

You deserve to feel happiness, Little Zoe. I wish that for you.

She had to keep going, think different thoughts.

Kayla walked past the alley where Naomi and Marcel set up their tent each night. Their tent was packed up and gone already, well before bylaw gave them trouble. But the space that belonged to that tent, where their well-worn welcome mat was laid out every night, felt homey.

There was the pawn shop with electronics and jewellery behind the grilled windows, along with a handwritten sign: *Yes, we probably have your bike.*

She continued past the ice cream parlour where a regular, Ice Cream Man, used to take her. And suddenly, another thought occurred. Far-fetched, but anything was possible. She remembered how she and Ice Cream Man would walk there, not holding hands, but close. He never talked on the way to ice cream. When they got there, he always murmured, *Take your time.* She was so surprised by the flow of their date—she was more used to providing the equivalent of a fast-food takeout meal—she had ordered the first thing she saw. *Don't rush,* he'd said.

That first date she had feared his fumbling, if his body would work and how she would console him when it did not. But he did not want to move from that bench. She'd thought, then, he must be paying for conversation, something to ease what she assumed were lonely days, but he barely answered her attempts. He seemed most content just to stare out at the water. Once he had reached towards her. His fingertips were cold and dry, papery. But he took his hand away, the graze of his fingertips almost gone before they had been there.

Another time he had reached out, staring somewhere above her ear, or at the air beside it. His hand was slow, as if he was afraid his hand might go through an apparition. He stopped before he made contact.

Then came that day when he said, *I have something for you.* With quivering hands, he took something out of a velvet pouch, held out a shaking fist. When he opened his hand there were two pearl earrings.

"Put them on. They were..."

They were heavy. They must have been real pearls.

She had started to reach towards her ears.

"No," he had said then, and it was the first time his voice had sounded stern. He raised his hand from where it sat against the fabric over his bony thighs. She thought he might hit her. He grabbed her wrist, surprisingly strong. She held her breath. But he just stared at her with unreadable eyes.

The next Friday he was not there, nor the one after. She thought he was done coming downtown. Then, one day, she saw him with Little Zoe, sitting on the same park bench. When she met up with Little Zoe and Cerise to get ready at Hearthstone later that evening, she noticed the earrings Little Zoe was removing from her ears before the evening began. Before she tucked them away in the jewellery box Nelson had salvaged for her, the one with the ballerina he said he could make dance again, Kayla noticed that Little Zoe had taken those pearls from the very first hole in her ears.

Could...?

So many thoughts traced back to her. Little Zoe was at once everywhere and nowhere.

I just want to find you.

Then, as she approached the corner, she saw Derek. He didn't have his fishing hat on, nor was his notebook open, so she figured he could talk.

"You see Little Zoe?"

"Haven't lately." Then his eyes brightened. "But actually, I did see a tiny girl with long blonde hair going into Hotel Zed earlier today. Just saw her from the back. But maybe it was her?"

Kayla gave him a quick hug of thanks, then beelined down the street towards the hotel.

Painted bright orange, purple, pink, and green, Hotel Zed promoted itself as a place of beachside fun. Today it had a sign out: *Valentine's Week Special – Rooms 11:00-2:00 for only $69!*

She rushed inside. Even from the scent of the cleaning products, even in the dim light, memory hit her.

The last time she'd been in there, she'd been brought by a man who drove a red minivan with lots of chrome, as though compensating for the sportscar he'd dreamed of in the 90s. After three tries inserting the electronic key into the door, with eyes both eager and nervous, he told her he wanted a duo.

"Do you have a friend?"

"Of course." It was important to have a friend at times like this. It was just a matter of finding out who that friend would be. Kayla and the man went out together, onto Leon, and found not just any friend but Little Zoe. Back in the hotel room, he paid them good money, said he wanted a show.

Little Zoe started asking him about his fantasies, getting him to draw out the details: just how that touch was, just where he wanted their mouths. She figured they could get even more if she took up extra time talking. There was a way she listened, as she had removed her shirt and sat there in her black lace bra, just the tiny swells of her breasts. Her jean skirt was too big around her waist.

They convinced him the show should start in the shower, both for extra time and to warm up. Little Zoe had licked her lips as she said, *Warm up*, her eyes half closed as if imagining how things would start to get steamy. But it was a cold day, and Kayla knew she meant warm up for real.

Little Zoe had a way of sliding her bra strap off her shoulder, unbuttoning the single button on her skirt.

Beside her, Kayla felt shy, novice, even though she had never been able to afford to be either.

Little Zoe went first, sliding down her skirt, letting the fabric of her bra grace her nipples. Then she turned, leaned forward at the waist. Slowly, slowly, she wriggled her thong to the floor.

Kayla had never seen Little Zoe naked before. She saw the cigarette burns, tiny circles in places teachers could not have reported. Little Zoe looked at Kayla's eyes, and she did not look away.

Little Zoe's hands were assured as she unhooked Kayla's bra, and brought her hands, then lips, over her breasts. Then the slow lowering of her thong with her teeth.

In the shower, the water was so good and hot, and the man stayed outside just to watch them. They told him his turn would come. Kayla could still smell the apple shampoo that they lathered on each other. Those silky wet touches.

Little Zoe knew how to use her tongue. She touched Kayla with so much tenderness it hurt—hurt because part of Kayla was there, more than just present inside herself, as she had vowed to be starting this work, to keep her wits about her. She was there.

With the water streaming, Little Zoe's hands on her hips, face between her legs, for a moment Kayla felt something more than just presence, and wondered if this is what pleasure could have been.

And then she truly let herself feel it. Feel it in all its force of emotion and all its gentleness. Truly feel it. Feel the gift Little Zoe was giving her and feel the beauty of receiving it.

And she was more truly there than she had ever been with another person. She was *there.*

That was my first time.

Tuesday, 10:00 a.m.

"Not here," the man at the hotel told her when Kayla tried to describe Little Zoe. "I've seen her before, sure, but not lately."

Kayla felt her heart sink. She stepped back out into the cold.

As she rounded towards City Park to ask her friends if anyone knew anything, Nelson stepped out of the alley. With his grizzled grey beard and doubled toques, his pale blue eyes were intent on Kayla.

"I found something. I think it belongs to Little Zoe." His voice was hoarse, as if he hadn't spoken out loud in a while. He fished into his pocket, then held out his hand, blackened from salvaging.

And there was the unicorn necklace Little Zoe always wore. Golden with a unicorn rearing up, with one leg outstretched. It was something a child might wear, but Little Zoe, who liked to believe in magic beyond what was supposed to exist, loved it.

"I found it in the park, at the shore."

Kayla looked at him, eyes widening.

"It's broken. But I can fix it. I just need a new part. I'll look out for one." He moved towards her. "I thought I'd give it to you, though, because I haven't seen her. You can give it to her."

Kayla sucked in her breath.

But it could mean nothing. The necklace was used. And things break. Things can break any time. Not necessarily because there was a struggle, anything wrong. Necklaces can simply break and fall in the sand. That could be all.

"I haven't seen her either," she told him. "But I will."

Trying not to think about what the necklace might mean, Kayla went in search of her friends, could hear them before she saw them: Mama B's laugh and the voices of Gloria, Naomi, Sally, Mel. So carefree and easy. So jarring against Kayla's worry, against the weight of the broken necklace in her hand.

Mama B and Gloria were sitting beside their carts. Naomi, Mel, and Sally were painting a bike. Buster supervised, wagging his tail when he saw Kayla.

Some bikes that came into the street community were found discarded, almost perfectly good. The one her friends were painting now would be shared around by people who needed to get somewhere. Folks out here made such finds their own. They changed more than just the colour. Depending on whatever paints they could get their hands on, they added flames, flowers, hearts, skulls, faces, eyes. Whatever someone could envision.

"Hey," Mel said, looking up. She had a bottle of nail polish in her hand, was creating the finer detail of a forest across the frame.

"Where you been?" Mama B asked. "We've been worried."

"I texted Ketchum and Cerise yesterday. Told them to tell you all." Not everyone had a phone. And then her own had run out of battery. "I stayed at Livia's. The outreach volunteer. Long story." And then the only question that mattered. "Has anyone heard anything about Little Zoe?"

"Nope," said Mama B.

"I hope she didn't have to leave town fast because she was in trouble," Sally said. Though new, Sally was learning how things ran.

"Or find trouble. Like up past Vernon," added Gloria. "I hear they have that guy on police watch." Although little was officially known, many people had their ideas about the missing women in the North Okanagan, the rumours about a farm where remains had been found. But processes were slow, inconclusive. And for some the justice system was only just in name.

"Personally, whenever I think of a woman gone missing, I can't help but think of that Nick guy with the boat," Naomi said.

Missing—the word made Kayla's stomach fall. Little Zoe was just...unaccounted for.

There had been rumours about a rich guy who'd taken a party boat out on the lake and a woman who never returned. Lots of people told of a wild party on the boat, but details of the night were blurry and varied. Some said her disappearance was just a coincidence, that she'd left the party before the boat left the dock, that she'd just left town. But some folks believed that Nick had done something horrible.

"Guys like that think street girls are expendable," Naomi said.

"Well, he has money," Mel said, "and his family has connections, so the cops aren't looking at him as hard as they should."

"In this town, you can get away with a lot if you have money," Mama B agreed.

"And if you're white," Gloria added.

Kayla nodded in agreement. She thought about telling them about the unicorn necklace, but she wanted to listen to what they had to say first. She wanted to see if anyone remembered anything more.

Just then, Kayla saw Cerise striding over. She was wearing her version of daytime casual: her look when working but when she didn't want to draw too much attention. She had on leggings and a zip-up hoodie she could unzip on the street if a potential client needed confirmation, ready to flash some lingerie or more.

"You hear anything from Little Zoe?" Kayla asked her before she sat down.

"No."

Kayla tried to read her friend's voice, wondering if Cerise was concerned, or if she were forcing herself to seem unconcerned, as if acting not worried meant there was nothing to worry about.

"But she has to come back," Cerise sighed. "Hearthstone's 48-hour policy and all. I already talked to them. They're willing to bend the rules a bit. For her. But it's been a while."

Hearthstone respected that a client's bed belonged to them, but an unoccupied bed meant someone else was going without. So if someone was not there for forty-eight hours, their bed had to become free.

"I was talking to other folks on Leon today," Mama B was saying. "Everyone said they'd keep an eye out. Derek said he'd look out for her when he rides the bus."

Derek liked to ride the bus—not to go to a particular destination, but just to ride the bus. It was a way of staying warm, and he liked to see other parts of the city, both to get away and for inspiration for his writing. He was ever watchful.

"Nelson found Little Zoe's unicorn necklace," Kayla finally blurted. "Broken. On the beach." She held it out for her friends to see.

"Oh my," said Sally.

"It could just be a coincidence," countered Mel.

"Yeah, anything can fall off like that," Mama B murmured, though Kayla saw worry in the old woman's eyes.

"Livia and Wanjiru filed a police report," Kayla told them. "I can text them and have them add this."

"You should," Mel agreed. "Just in case."

Kayla pulled her phone from her pack and started texting.

Just then, they saw Lily striding over, needling through the park from the direction of Leon. Rather than dressed for work, she was in her fluorescent-striped construction snow pants, perhaps a gift from a customer. Her hair was in pigtails, messy from the night before. Lily was experienced enough to capitalize on her youth.

"Kayla's looking for Little Zoe," Mama B told her. "You know anything?"

"No," Lily said, pacing and hardly looking at them. "You got anything that can tide me over? I'm too fucking dope sick to work."

But no one had anything to help her out. Not the kind of help she needed. Gloria gave her a candy from the outreach volunteers, something for her blood sugar at least. She started to cry. "I need to fucking work then. Fuck. I can't work like this. But I have to."

She struggled to peel out of her snow pants. She had last night's dress underneath. When she took off her coat, her bandages were falling off her arm. Her sore was weeping through the gauze.

"Let me redo those for you at least," Mama B said, eyeing up the stained bandages, the swelling. Burgundy streaked up Lily's inner elbow.

Gloria had gauze from the outreach volunteers in her cart. Together, they worked on Lily's shaking arm. How different she was from the girl who had found an abandoned soccer ball in the park one day, started bouncing it on her knee and doing tricks, rounded them all up to play. It was hard to imagine she was the same girl. But she was. She was both.

When they were done wrapping Lily's arm, Lily fumbled in her purse and got her eyeshadow, which she shakily spread across her eyelids. They sparkled like dead butterfly wings.

Kayla felt numb with worry for Little Zoe, but everyone else just resumed talking like thing were fine. People did just drop out of the scene for a bit sometimes, after all. But then they came back.

Across the park, she saw Kori coming towards them. For once Kayla was glad to see her.

"Kori!" she called. "Just wondering if you remembered any more about Little Zoe the other night? Anything about that black car?"

"What black car?"

"The one you saw Little Zoe get into?"

"Black car? I don't remember shit about a black car." She shrugged. Then she half smiled. "But I did find her hoodie. Here, in the park. By the beach. The one with the angel wings."

Kayla's heart raced.

"Ten dollars and it's yours. And there's a picture in the pocket, too."

"Fuck, Kori! Just give it to me. We don't know where she is. Don't fuck around."

"Ten dollars. Firm."

Kayla had the money in her bra but suddenly found her hand across Kori's face. Hard.

"What the fuck?" Kori held her lip.

"Give it! Fucking give it!" She was surprised at her own voice.

"You crazy bitch." But Kori rummaged in her pack. And sure enough, she came out with Little Zoe's hoodie, its angel wings glittering.

Kayla held the fabric to her face and breathed in Little Zoe's perfume. She could feel the photograph inside the pocket. When she pulled it out, there was a younger version of Little Zoe, fuller faced, hair dark. But her eyes were the same—the way the one eye turned into a crescent moon when she smiled. And she was smiling in the photograph. Smiling big and real. She was with a woman who had a perm from another era, though the photo must have been taken more recently than that, judging by Little Zoe's age. They were carving a pumpkin, a bowl of scooped pulp and seeds beside them. The pumpkin had triangle eyes but no mouth yet, but the look on the girl's face was pure happiness.

Kayla flipped the photograph over. An address was written in ink: 46 River Street, Hope, BC.

"Last time I talked to her, she said she was going to do something special," Kori said then.

Kayla's heart skipped. "What? When did you talk to her?"

"I don't know. Not too long ago."

Kayla looked at her with pleading eyes, wanting something more, but Kori couldn't give it.

"Something special is all she said."

Tuesday, Noon

Kayla had enough money in her bra—earnings from her night with the man in the suburbs—to pay for bus fare to Hope. The town was three hours away, across the bridge and through the mountains towards Vancouver, but it was the one lead she had.

The bus was warm enough to fog the windows against the cold outside. Waiting in her seat, she looked at the address on the back of the photo. Her hopes tremored. She wanted something, anything. Could something special await her friend in a town called, of all things, Hope?

The bus pulled out from its parking bay and threaded out of downtown, past the doorways of businesses where Kayla had slept and past the alleyways in which she had worked so many days and nights. She looked out as they went over the bridge, past billboards and strip malls and into the hills. Sagebrush and rust-coloured rock faces gave way to pine forests and mountains. Kayla hoped, hard as she could hope, that was the route Little Zoe had taken on her way to a different life. That there was something good to go back to and that she had found it. It was better than thinking about what the hoodie and broken necklace might mean. Kayla had already updated Livia and Wanjiru. They were going to meet with the cops again today—better them than her.

Perhaps Little Zoe had reconnected with an old foster parent? Growing up in the foster care system, she had been scuttled from family to family, although only a few felt like real families. But from the picture there had been something good once. Sure, Kayla had seen the scars of cigarette burns on Little Zoe's body. And like Kayla, she had other less visible scars too. Yet in the photograph Kayla now held, Little Zoe was smiling for real. Whoever this woman she was with was, there was a home there, or had been.

Kayla tried to conjure hope, to stoke it as much as she could, as the bus continued through misty, pine-cloaked mountains and frozen waterfalls, all under a pale winter sky.

When the driver announced that they were pulling into Hope, Kayla felt a surge of excitement, though the small town didn't look like much. There was a gas station with a convenience store and a sign that said *BUS*, a few people with bags waiting beside it. Further down the street were a man and a woman, both layered in coats, hoods pulled up, smoking. They had a shopping cart beside them, heaped, with a tarp over top.

The cold air was a bracing contrast from the bus. She headed to the convenience store, holding the photograph. It had never made it to her pocket. The turbaned clerk knew the address, directed her down the road past the Thunderbird Motel.

She walked past a stretch of modest houses, empty fields, bungalows with paint peeling off their siding, rusted pickup trucks in the front yards, until finally coming to River Street. She could see number 46 as soon as she turned the corner. She sucked in her breath, approached the busted screen door, and rang the bell. There was frenzied barking from inside. Footsteps. A woman, grey hair framing her face, opened the door, staring at Kayla with questioning eyes. But she was not an older version of the woman in the photograph.

"Hi. I'm looking for my friend." Kayla held out the photograph. "The picture I have has this address on it. You know her?"

The woman reached forward, studied the photo, and furrowed her brow. "Well, the woman there, I do know. Rented this place before me. But they've been gone a while, eh? She had this house full of kids she took in. Like I do." Kayla could hear cartoons coming from inside, smelled Kraft Dinner on the stove.

"The girl, though—" Kayla tried. "Did she ever come here? Recently? Maybe looking for someone?"

The woman shook her head. "Just me and the kids. But if you think she's in town you could try the Thunderbird. Yeah. Actually, I think that girl used to sneak into the tavern there. A ways back. Underage, but they pretended different sometimes. You could check there."

Kayla returned the photo to her pocket, feeling empty. If Little Zoe hadn't been to the house, it was unlikely she'd been to Hope at all. Which meant the other possibilities of where she might be loomed again. Kayla didn't want to think of it. But she would go to the tavern, just in case.

The bar at the motel, with its stucco façade and a couple of pickup trucks out front, wasn't far. It smelled of stale beer and fried food. When her eyes adjusted to the dimness, she could see a couple of men sitting at opposite ends of the bar. She took a bar stool in the centre. The man to her right had a trucker's hat on and a nearly empty pint, alongside a plate of chicken-wing bones. He looked at her with interest as the bartender came from the back.

"What can I get you?" the bartender asked.

She handed him the photo. "I'm looking for my friend. The girl on the left. Have you seen her? She has long blonde hair now."

When the bartender looked down at the photo, something flashed across his face. "She used to come here."

The man beside Kayla raised his empty pint glass, gesturing for more.

"Nice girl," the bartender said as he pulled the man his pint. "Left town though, a while back. Haven't seen her in years."

She stared at the photo, tracing it with her finger, and couldn't help but feel her anxiety rising. She stared down at the bar, into the grain of the wood.

"You just in town to see about your friend, or are you looking for a little something more?"

Although the man with the chicken bones had a mustache, she didn't get cop vibes. He had a creased face, a lingering smell of smoke. But he was likely staying here at the hotel. He'd have a warm room, maybe a bathtub. Certainly a shower. And first, he might order more food. The strange, welcome comfort of work washed over her then. She wanted to feel anything but the rising panic of Little Zoe's absence.

"Brian," he said, sticking out his hand. His fingers were slightly sticky.

"Desiree."

"I know your friend, Desiree." He glanced at the photograph, swigged. "Might just be able to help you find her."

*

The forest service road winding up the mountain was barely gravel, pocked with potholes and the uneven melting and freezing of early spring snow. Thick walls of pines flanked both sides. The crackling radio faded into static as they climbed.

It was stupid, she knew. She had broken her own rule. It had been Little Zoe who taught her the rules when Kayla had first arrived in Kelowna: take the johns to the well-lit parking lot of City Park, or work in the alleyways where other street folks were able to hear you, just in case. Work in motels was a given, but you had your phone, and could usually count on thin walls. But a forest service road in the middle of nowhere—with no cell signal—that was different.

After she'd agreed to go with him, he'd ended up saying he wasn't staying at the motel after all—there would be no hot shower for her—but she felt desperate enough, in so many ways, that she had gone with him anyway.

"She's probably at Dougie's," he'd told her. "Liked to party there. Bet she's there. I'll take you just after..."

So stupid and she knew it. But at the mention of Little Zoe, logic crumbled.

And it could be true: maybe Little Zoe knew somewhere else in town where she might find the woman in the picture, and had been here in town after all. Maybe she'd stopped to earn some money, or for a fix, before seeking her out.

"Yep, I bet you that she's gone to Dougie's to party," he'd said. "That was always her favourite. You'll see. It'll be a good time."

Kayla had come all this way. She wanted something to hang onto. Anything.

The man's hands smelled like honey garlic chicken wings when he reached towards her face. The vinyl seat was cold against her naked hip. Her dress was raised, but her boots were on. She had insisted he pay her before they began. But the way his fingers encircled her wrist after he came, those fingers too tight around her, too insistent and unyielding, made the feeling in her stomach go from bad to worse.

She looked at his eyes and knew she had to flee.

That he went to lock the truck when she reached for the door handle only confirmed her fears.

"You think we're done?"

But she managed to crack the door before the locks went down, sprang out and ran into the forest, the thick forest where the truck couldn't go, thrashing through branches, her boots crunching through the hardened snow, running deeper and deeper into the forest before he could follow. She heard him yelling from the road, then footsteps crashing in the snow after her.

Eventually she stopped hearing the footsteps, but her own feet never stopped.

No one knew she was here. She'd left so quickly that she hadn't told Cerise, hadn't texted Ketchum. She was just another girl running in the forest, like in a horror movie. *This is how it happens,* she thought, boots crunching in the snow, lungs aching, the branches above no protection.

Breath ragged, mist spilling from her mouth into the winter air, she just kept running in the direction where she hoped the road might be. Eventually, hearing nothing but her own breath and the silence of the forest, not even a bird above, she slowed to a walk. She walked until she could hear the distant rumble of trucks' air brakes, the hiss of traffic. Then she headed towards the gas station with the bus stop. But she didn't get there.

She found, on her way, the man and woman she had seen when she got off the bus, with their brimming shopping cart covered with a tarp. Kayla recognized in the way they stood, braced against the wind, those who knew the street. She recognized in their eyes not just the dilated glint of drugs but a familiarity, a familiarity that on this day was a strange comfort. She saw in their eyes those who knew what it was to sleep rough, with one eye open, open for yourself and for those who had become your family. There was a familiarity and strange comfort there. A comfort that gave her hope that Little Zoe might still be found, that lessened the grip of the man in the truck, that reminded her of the folks on the street back home—that's how she thought of it, in her head, she realized—*home.* A comfort that she needed badly just now.

Perhaps that was why she went with the couple through the snow, behind a boarded-up bungalow, past the browned carcasses of an overgrown garden poking through crystalline ice, and to a shed at the back of the property. It was an old tool shed that was falling in on itself. Paint was peeling off it in strips. Moss cloaked what was left of the roof.

The man banged on the shack's door with his fist. It opened. Kayla followed him inside. Among the rusted paint tins, old tools, and heaps of blankets and garbage, were needles.

When the man asked her if she wanted something—something she had been asked so many times—she stopped and looked at him.

Those back home on Leon had asked this question again and again, with the strange cordiality of the street, before they learned that she would always say no. Those who came cruising by on bikes, who didn't know her but thought they knew the type, asked too, hissing, *Want uppers? Want down?* Always, she had said, *No.*

But this time, after she had held onto that worn photo like a beacon and a talisman, after she had felt her hopes soar and plummet, at the home in the address, and again with the chicken bone man's promise that he knew Little Zoe—how those hopes crashed along with the hard-held practices by which she survived—and after what might have happened on the forest service road, after she thought of how no one would even know if it had, after she thought of how easy it is to disappear, how untraceable, how so much just felt untraceable and overwhelming and hopeless, so fucking hopeless, hopeless, hopeless, she paused.

And then she said the word that surprised her.

"Yes."

She didn't know if the man was motivated by simple generosity towards a stranger who seemed to have a need he understood or if he just wanted the money in her bra. She just recognized a look in his eyes that she knew, and that knew her. A comfort and familiarity that she so desperately needed on this hopeless day.

So when he asked her, she said, "Yes."

She put away the photograph for the last time that day.

She took off her coat, held out her arm.

She said, "Yes, I'm sure."

And his hand was sure with the needle.

Then her body was saying yes to a flooding heat, a calm, a tranquility that she already knew but no longer cared was fleeting, would turn in on itself. It rushed into her with a powerful insistence, a strange comfort. A feeling that she could at least have this.

She thought of Little Zoe.

*

What was the feeling Little Zoe had sought? Was it to feel so intensely, so fully, or to feel not at all?

What...

*

She was cold, bordering of numbness. She stirred, not opening her eyes, reaching for herself. Her hand, so cold it burned, felt the skin of her icy hip.

She snapped her eyes open.

She was naked. She was alone in a room with a small white square of window, a seam of light at the bottom of the door. Underneath her body, she could feel the cold of the cracked linoleum floor of the shed, the frozen earth beneath.

Her clothes were strewn on the floor beside her, along with spent needles.

She was sore—acutely and throughout her body. She felt at once empty and too full, sick in a way she had never felt before. Terrified she didn't know what had happened.

Little Zoe, she murmured, but she didn't even know if she were speaking out loud. Reality felt blurred. She didn't know what she needed to tell her friend, what she needed to ask. Just that she did. That she needed to reach out in some way. But all she could say was, *Little Zoe.*

*

After she had put her clothes back on—they were not torn as she had feared—she didn't know if that made it worse—she had opened the door of the shack and stepped out into the blinding white cold. She walked to the bus stop, watched her feet move across the sidewalk with its ice and salt and ingrained grime. Each step was heavy. Heavy like the broken necklace in her pocket.

But despite feeling foggy and used up, her thoughts couldn't help but turn towards what she would do when she got back to Kelowna. Where she would look, who she could possibly ask? Her fingers played with the corner of the photograph in her pocket, enigmatic as it was useless.

But it wasn't useless. No—it showed Little Zoe smiling, a genuinely happy moment—and beyond showing what had been, it showed what *could* be. That Little Zoe was capable of such genuine happiness. And could be again.

By the time the sun was sinking behind the mountains, the bus was pulling away, its hum a lullaby if she transformed it enough, leaving behind the gas station and convenience store, the mouth of a forest service road, the man who had held the needle, and the woman who'd moaned, *Oh honey*, when she saw Kayla's pristine inner arms.

Tuesday, 9:00 p.m.

When the bus pulled into Kelowna, Kayla stared out at the city with different eyes. After what happened in Hope—after what she had done—her body and mind felt eaten up. She felt the urge to use again. She had done it once, felt she had nothing left to lose. The lullaby of the bus was gone, disintegrated too, and she just felt a gnawing.

Maybe Little Zoe and Cerise were onto something. Maybe the surge was worth it, could numb the pain enough. She wondered if, in a world where so little felt guaranteed, you could at least guarantee a feeling. A fleeting feeling, but a feeling all the same.

She took in the darkened streets with their sunken snow grimy with road salt, the buildings with their closed doors, the footprints frozen in the ice. The alleys.

She reached into her pocket—the photo of Little Zoe and the woman was now in her pack—and felt for the broken unicorn necklace. Its metal was cold.

By this hour Cerise would have worked enough to get the fix she needed. Kayla figured she might be able to find her friend in an alley. She stepped down from the bus and walked, listening to her own footsteps and not caring. And sure enough she found Cerise.

Cerise's eyes, pupils dilated wide, widened more when Kayla asked her.

"But you don't use." She had the needle in her hand. But she just stared at Kayla.

"I want to now. Fuck it."

"But Kayla—"

"I said I want to. Share like a good friend."

Cerise didn't move.

"I'll pay. Here." Kayla fished out the remaining cash from her bra and handed it over. "If you're running out, we can go score more in a minute, okay? Just share with me. Fucking share with me."

Kayla saw her friend's face flicker with emotions: resistance, and then, as Cerise realized it could be something they could share together, something like camaraderie. And that Kayla could buy.

Cerise got the needle ready. Kayla took off her coat, rolled up her sleeve as she had done before. The air was cold and biting, and she welcomed it, as if to match the pain.

Cerise looked Kayla in the eyes, checking to see she really meant it, and reached forward with the needle.

"What the fuck!"

From out of nowhere, Ketchum was there in the alley. Before Kayla could take in what was happening, he had grabbed the needle from Cerise. He shoved it in his own hand. Right on the back of his hand.

"For fuck's sake, Kayla," he hissed. "Don't do this. Fucking don't. Whatever you do, just fucking don't."

He looked at her, his eyes hard with warning, and slid the empty needle from his hand.

Tuesday, 10:00 p.m.

Kayla listened to her footsteps on the sidewalk as she walked towards the *t'st'siłp* tree in the park.

After Ketchum had taken the needle himself, he had hugged her, sobbing. "Promise me. Just don't. Don't ruin what you have. Promise me."

And she did have so much to live for. Painful as it could be sometimes. "I promise."

He held her eyes.

"I promise." She pulled away. "But I need to go to my tree. Just need to be myself for a while."

Yet when she got to her tree, someone was under it already. She could see their cart, shoes sticking out from the branches.

She stared at *t'st'siłp* and realized she didn't want to be there, not like that. She felt tainted. *t'st'siłp* was a sacred space. After today, she felt she didn't deserve to be there. Not just then. One sacred place had already been tainted. She didn't want to taint this one too. She could at least prevent that.

Walking towards her usual corner, she approached the Safeway parking lot. The grocery store was closed, but there was a lone car there, under the falling snow. Beside it was Livia.

"You're crying," Livia called over, gently, when she saw her. "What's wrong?"

So much to tell. But she just felt quiet.

"I was going to grab a coffee," Livia tried. "Want to join me?"

It wasn't what Kayla really needed. If she were going to be around anyone she should have stayed with Ketchum. But here she was.

So she and Kayla went to the only coffee shop that was open. Under the fluorescent lights Livia's hair was messy, eyes glassy. Kayla could smell alcohol on her breath.

"Anything else with that?" asked the woman behind the counter, when Livia ordered her coffee.

"No thanks."

"We have a sandwich," the woman continued. "Someone paid but didn't take it. You can have it. For free." She reached into the cooler where the sodas and sandwiches were.

Livia looked confused. But Kayla recognized the look of pity on the woman's face.

"No thanks, I'm fine." Livia looked flustered. Then she turned to Kayla. "You want it?"

"Sure," Kayla said. She looked at her friend and knew Livia had seen what she must look like, who she was assumed to be.

As they stepped outside and headed towards the parking lot, Kayla unwrapped the sandwich and took a hesitant bite, not sure what she needed in her body just then. Nothing felt right.

"Any new information?"

Kayla just shook her head.

They walked in silence to where Livia was parked.

"I really liked talking with you that day you came over," Livia said, unlocking the car and motioning for Kayla to come in. She cranked the heater. "I was thinking...you said you liked taking pictures? Am I remembering that right? Maybe we could take some together sometime? Out here? Or in the hills by my house?"

"I'd like that," Kayla said slowly, appreciating even just the modicum of heat. She realized, then, that she would like that. She cherished the photos she had of Buddy and her grandma and her fuzzy outline of a dad. And the one of Little Zoe when she was younger, looking happy, possibly before anything truly bad had happened. Taking pictures would let her record new memories of the friends and the life she was making.

"I'd really like that too," Livia continued. "It would get me back at it, maybe. And I could give you my old camera if you'd like."

"My phone is fine for pictures. And I need to carry everything I have with me. Thanks though."

They watched the snow as it caught in the triangle cast by a streetlight.

"There's another thing I wanted to tell you," Livia said, slowly. "I want to stop drinking. I'm sure you've noticed. But I want to stop. Need to stop. I...I'm going to try. Soon."

She put her coffee cup in the cup holder, beside an empty mug with a dark circle of wine at the bottom. "Do you want to come back to my place?"

The promise of warmth, and a bed, beckoned. But after not finding Little Zoe, after all that had happened, after she had used and tried to use again—and the shame that came with it, the awful possibilities—she didn't want comfort. The difficulty of the night seemed to demand the difficulty of the street. As much as she wanted to go, she also didn't want to go with Livia. She needed to be by herself. She needed to figure out just who herself was right now.

And she needed to be with her people. Find Mama B or Gloria or Naomi and Marcel, maybe share a tent and a hug from someone who had been here too.

"I'm alright," Kayla told her, reaching for her backpack and then the handle of the car's door. "Honest. Just go home. You have a home to go to."

But so did Kayla.

Wednesday, 7:30 a.m.

"Hey, Kayla, I heard where Little Zoe was going. Mama B said you were looking."

Tyler leaned over the handlebars of his bike, hoodie pulled up. He stared over her from where she was curled in her sleeping bag on the sidewalk, under an opaque morning sky. Naomi and Marcel, Gloria, and Mama B had been quiet in their tents by the time Kayla got back to Leon the night before. As much as she wanted their company, needed her family, she hadn't wanted to wake them. But just knowing they were there was something.

"What?"

"Yeah. I know about Little Zoe. Thought I'd tell ya."

Kayla's heart was racing. "What do you know?"

"She might have gone with someone Jason knows." Tyler straightened his shoulders with importance, pleased to be the one with something someone wanted for once. "I can take you."

"Yes." She was afraid to feel even a bit of hope, but did anyway. "Please."

He held himself slightly taller on his bike. "You want to sit on my handlebars?"

Tyler put her pack on his own back and Kayla climbed on, a bit awkwardly given her bad hip. Then they pedalled down Leon and out of downtown. They headed north up the highway, past hotels and chain restaurants and the mall. The man with the cowboy hat and the baby trailer attached to his bike, filled with empty cans and bottles, whipped past. As Kayla and Tyler continued, going by strip plazas and light industrial, along came a man with a train of three carts strung together by rope, moving along the sidewalk with all he owned and the recycling he had collected.

The wind carried a hint of spring warmth as it rushed by Kayla's face. She hadn't ridden on anyone's handlebars since she was a kid.

"I'll take you to where Jason is," he said. "But I just gotta make a stop at Tent City."

There was a place behind Enterprise Road, along the Rail Trail, in the forest and thickets behind the car dealerships and discount stores, where many unhoused folks made their homes. Trails and a river wound through those thick woods. There it was possible to live in the city but not in the city, to be tucked away on its margins. It was a place where you could live by your own means and on your own terms—until bylaw came and told you to move along. Ketchum lived there sometimes, fashioning places to live out of discarded wood pallets from the big-box store parking lots nearby. His places were always temporary, ready to be taken down as soon as bylaw made a sweep. But he could always rebuild. He helped others do so too.

"You seriously have to stop?" She wanted to get to wherever Jason was as soon as possible. But she didn't know where they were going. She had to stick with Tyler. And he had been kind, bringing her out here like this.

"It'll just take a sec. Just have to make a delivery."

Kayla followed Tyler down a path between a car dealership and a mattress company, then into the woods. Tyler walked over to an especially tall, graffitied tree, where someone's cart was parked. A meeting place.

Kayla hoped whatever Tyler was doing wouldn't take long. He smoked while they waited.

Looking through the naked branches of cottonwood and aspen that flanked the trail, Kayla could see tents pitched in the woods. Laundry hung on a line between trees. A tendril of smoke rose from a campfire. Come spring, when the trees and bushes leafed out, this place would be filled with even more ideal hiding spots to live. Where you could find your own place. Or try.

The path curled alongside the river, which was already alive with spring thaw. The sounds of rushing water drowned out the drone of the highway. A pair of ducks floated along where the water met the ice. Kayla watched the ducks as they waited and waited. Tyler didn't have a phone so there was no way to know if anyone was actually coming.

Three cigarettes later, he picked up his bike. "I guess my friend's not making it."

She and Tyler continued down the trail, tree branches swaying above, dark against the paleness of the sky.

They approached a shelter someone had built in the woods. Their shopping cart, loaded and covered with another tarp, was a supporting wall.

"Hello, Stan," Tyler called, getting off his bike and walking towards the shelter. Kayla saw a man sitting on a wooden pallet beside it. He had a knife and something else in his hands. Wearing a toque and bulky layers of coats, grimy from sleeping rough, he was unshaven. He was old in that ageless, ancient way some street people became in the elements. Kayla didn't recognize him as anyone she had ever seen downtown.

"Afternoon," the man eventually said. He stood, holding the knife and a piece of wood. He put it them down and then reached for a broken cardboard box and a couple of sticks, which he placed on the charred remains of a campfire, lit with a lighter. Flame snaked up the cardboard and eventually caught the wood. The man pulled over another pallet beside the one on which he had been sitting, and motioned for Kayla and Tyler to sit.

"Make yourself at home." Then he picked up the knife and piece of wood he had been holding.

"You carving?" Tyler asked.

The man nodded and held up a piece of wood that was turning into an eagle.

"The trees told me what this one wanted to be." Though his voice was gruff, his words were different than what Kayla had first imagined. There was a brightness in his eyes.

"Sometimes I sell them on the street," he said, looking at Kayla. "Walk up to people in cars stopped at traffic lights. Most people shake their heads or tell me to fuck off, but a few people see what the wood wanted to become." He stroked the eagle. "But sometimes they are to keep. I make them because the wood tells me there's a story within it, something wanting to come out and make itself known."

He began to carve again, shavings of wood falling at his feet. They sat around the fire, watching it burn. It gave off the faintest trace of warmth.

It felt good for Kayla to sit. She wanted to catch up with Jason, find out what he knew, but it was so peaceful here. She could hear the steady flow of the creek, louder than the distant traffic. Above them, the spring's first birds were flitting from branch to branch. One carried something in their beak, as if gathering the beginnings of a nest.

She remembered the forest where she had ridden Buddy, what seemed so long ago. The wind in the trees, the music of the river.

Kayla watched the man's hands work and wondered about the stories he saw in the wood. Perhaps out here it would be easier to hear those stories, to feel connected with the land, to be a part of something more than just the city. Perhaps he came out here not because he had nowhere else to be, but because he felt that connection more strongly than anywhere else.

"My friend here is looking for a girl," Tyler said at last, his voice an interruption in the quiet. "Little Zoe. She's real little. Long blonde hair. You know her?"

The man did not look up from his work, but shook his head. "I'll keep an eye out."

Kayla didn't know why Tyler thought the man might know Little Zoe. They led such different existences. She also did not know why they had come to this man. But as Tyler stared at the fire and at the man's art, she saw that something was changed about him. There was almost a peace within him that she had not seen before. Tyler lived by his own music and perhaps out here he could hear it more clearly.

The man continued to carve. The fire continued to burn.

"Well thanks then," Tyler said eventually, standing.

"Yes, thanks," Kayla said, wondering if she was thanking the man for looking out for Little Zoe, or for the warming fire and the feeling she had in these woods. She stood.

The man looked up from his eagle and watched as made their way through the bush.

Stepping through the twigs and last year's fallen leaves, Kayla thought of what it would be like to stay out here, to sleep in this forest instead of on the streets. Come summer, along with the rushing of the creek, she imagined there would be crickets, just like there had been at the farm. And perhaps, in time, the crickets would become sweet, peaceful music once again. Not the screaming they had been on the night she left, as she had continued down that dark road, but just crickets in the grasses, singing their songs of night. A sweet and peaceful music that perhaps she could learn to hear again.

Wednesday, 1:00 p.m.

After winding out of the woods and to the road, Kayla hopped back up on Tyler's handlebars. There was a trace of warmth in the wind rushing against her face.

They went past hotels and fast-food joints and plazas, past the new supportive housing units in a converted old motel. A number of people from the street had moved here, a secure a spot after staying at shelters. Someone had hung a dreamcatcher in one of the windows.

Tyler eventually turned into the Rutland neighbourhood, with its low-rise apartment buildings and bungalows, old cars and well-loved pickup trucks in driveways. They went past old women pushing laundry hampers and young women pushing strollers. Some yards had plastic kiddie slides, or carcasses of last year's marigolds and geraniums. Tinfoil was placed over one window; in another was a child's drawing of a rainbow and a Canadian flag.

Tyler stopped at an old bungalow with boarded-up windows. The fence around it had broken pickets like missing teeth. Kayla followed Tyler as he knocked on the door. After a moment the lock slid. A man with bulging, tattooed biceps opened it, but blocked the doorway.

"She's here to talk to Jason," Tyler said. "She's fine."

The man mumbled something but stepped aside. They went down the staircase into a basement room, Tyler carrying his bike. The ceiling felt too low.

Jason and a man Kayla didn't know were at a folding table. Their drug paraphernalia was spread in front of them, plus scales and bottles of pills. Kayla recalled that Little Zoe had once said she learned decimals and fractions not in school but from dealing drugs.

In one corner was a ripped old recliner chair, and on the other side of the room was a worn couch. A guy covered in blankets, with his hoodie pulled over his face, lay there, out.

"My man," Tyler said, going to fist bump Jason.

Jason's face said Tyler was far from his man.

Jason was prison fit, having spent his time doing push-ups in isolation after meting out justice from someone who'd done him wrong. Jason's pit bull was at his feet, wearing his dog coat.

The third man, lean with a tattoo on his face, looked at Kayla and smiled.

"Welcome to my humble abode. Want a drink? Or maybe something else?"

Kayla shook her head. "I just came to ask Jason something. I heard a friend of mine might've been here. Little Zoe. I heard you guys might know where she is."

"She's not here," Jason said.

"Didn't she say she was going up past Vernon?" the man with the tattoo on his face asked.

Up past Vernon. Where women had gone missing. Where remains had been found on a farm.

"I don't fucking know," Jason snarled.

"Tyler said she went with someone you know?"

"I know a lot of people."

The other man shrugged. "Yeah, I think she was going to meet some guy who lived by the lake? Some rich party guy? Seemed like it was going to be good money." He motioned towards the recliner. "I can text a couple people. My friend Mandy might know. You can stay and wait if you want."

Kayla decided she might as well appreciate the warmth while she waited for any news. Sometimes there was a price to pay for staying somewhere warm for a while, but neither of the guys gave her that look that demanded payment in kind. They were busy preparing their drugs.

Tyler tried to chat them up, be part of it all, but they just did their thing. So he just kept pulling out his glass pipe, sucking himself into another place but seemingly not quite finding where he wanted to be. The sense of peace she'd sensed from him in the woods was gone.

Her own sense of peace had dwindled too. As the tiny rectangular basement window grew dark, worry ate at Kayla. She kept checking her phone, but still nothing from Little Zoe.

Eventually the man who had been lying facedown on the couch, covered up, stirred. Kayla saw it was Ketchum.

Feeling surged through her as she recalled the night before.

Ketchum opened his eyes but didn't seem present there in that room. He had a way of looking haunted. Perhaps not surprising for someone who had worked the kill floor of a slaughterhouse. And then there had been his girlfriend who overdosed, who came to him with messages in streetlights, in the eyes of the ducks on Leon, in graffiti. And before that, his family from long ago. And surely layers beyond that about which Kayla didn't know.

Ketchum looked up and saw her.

"Kayla." He sat. He looked at her, eyes hard and soft all at once. "You—you—never do that again—"

"I already promised you." It felt a lifetime ago.

"Don't promise unless you mean it."

"You have my word." She sat beside him on the couch.

Jason looked over at them from the table.

Ketchum stood. "Let's go outside."

They climbed the stairs and went out into what someone could have turned into a backyard. In the fading light, they sat on mildew-spotted camp chairs.

"There's still nothing on Little Zoe. I don't know what to do." She tried to keep her voice as steady as she could.

"There's not always something you *can* do. Sometimes it just is what it is." His voice was more comforting, less fatalist than his words were.

Kayla nodded slowly, but her mind was racing. She thought back to that evening she and Little Zoe had shared on Dilworth Mountain. "Maybe she went to go find her daughters."

"That's not always so easy." He took a moment, not looking at her, and his eyes misted over. Kayla knew he'd lost his first family in those days his addiction had controlled him, and he still missed them fiercely. Sometimes that missing was what drove him back into the hell that had caused it, using as if to erase the pain. He saw photographs of his daughter on social media every so often. He had watched her grow up from a distance, though he had never stopped caring.

"Hard as it can be, sometimes it's better to let them go on without you," he said finally. "It can seem like a good idea to reconnect, but sometimes it's better, for them at least, if you let them lead their life..."

"But you said you wish you could be there for your daughter."

"As a parent, all you want is what's best for your child."

"But don't you want to be there—"

He took a long pause. "Sometimes I do. And other times I know I'm better staying away. But I do want to be there. I am there in my own way."

She looked at him.

"I've done a lot of living. I have a lot of stories to tell, mistakes to learn from, wisdom to share. So I write to her. I don't send those letters to her, though. But if it's meant to be, she'll read my words some day. Maybe even hear my voice. Maybe even..." He looked far away. "Or maybe I'll just burn those letters up finally. Or who knows—maybe I just haven't written the right ones for her yet. But forcing something, especially when the time isn't right, that's no good. If it's meant to happen it will."

Kayla nodded, considering. She recalled the day Little Zoe had seen her daughter in the pizza place.

"She wants to get them back someday. She could be a great mother, if she was clean. She has a lot of love to give."

"She does. And she's young. Not like me. And you're right—she does have a lot of love to give. And...and you—you love her very much."

"I do."

He didn't look away. "All of these things are possible. But Kayla...you have to consider other possibilities, too. You can't deny that she might be gone."

Gone.

Ketchum's words began to sink in, as much as she didn't want to let them.

She had to face that possibility.

Gone.

Sometime in the Night

And in time, Ketchum too was gone. As Jason and his crew packed up, he'd stayed around, chatting and trying to cheer Kayla up, to be there for her as he could. He didn't want to bring her down, he said, just let her be aware so she wasn't shocked if something had happened. For a while, it worked. He knew how to make her laugh. Her spirits raised. In that apartment, she warmed up for real—*a good defrost,* as Little Zoe liked to joke.

But then: *Gone.*

The spectre kept creeping back.

"You going to be okay?" Ketchum asked her as Jason and his crew were putting their product in backpacks, tucking in the weigh scale. She saw that Ketchum was packing up too, putting his coat on over his hoodie, pulling up his hood. He never stayed in one place too long. Things to do, places to be. Both the ways of the street and a restless energy called him. As did disappearing into the woods. And he especially didn't like to stay in one place after softening into memory. She knew, respected that.

"I hope you find her. I'll be thinking of you both. But I've got to go."

"I know."

"But you'll be alright."

"I will be," Kayla said. "I will be."

Not going to be downtown tonight, she texted Cerise. *Any sign of Little Zoe?*

Eventually: *No.*

Kayla realized she was exhausted. Last night had been sleepless, for sure, but she was more exhausted with not knowing.

She figured she would feel it if her phone buzzed, if she kept it close. So she got her sleeping bag from her pack and crawled inside. Banishing all thoughts from her mind, in that way only possible after true exhaustion, she eventually fell into a deep sleep. She even drifted into a dream. In that way dreams made no sense and sense all at once, Demi Ray was there, and so was

Little Zoe. There was the sound of frogs, and, despite the coldness of the basement room in which she slept, crickets and a soothing summer wind.

But sometime in the night, Jason was standing over her with his phone, its screen lit up. Mandy had texted back.

Yeah, saw Little Zoe a few days ago. She said she was going with that guy we met in the summer. Who liked to party on his boat. But I didn't go. Sketchy as fuck. People say he took a girl out on a boat and she didn't come back. I think she was going to go though? Crazy girl!

"Text her back," Kayla said. "See if you can get details."

His name is Nate. Has a place on the lake.

Kayla entered Mandy's number into her own phone. Her throat felt tight.

This is Zoe's friend. Do you have an address? she texted.

I can get one. I'll text you back.

Grabbing her pack, Kayla climbed the stairs and quietly stepped into the predawn cold. She headed towards the main street, with its apartment buildings, its businesses waiting to open for the day. Snow had started overnight and was covering the ground. Big fluffy flakes caught in her eyelashes and hair.

Please text me, she wrote to Little Zoe. Her hands were shaking, and not just from the cold.

You awake? she texted Cerise. *Text me back.*

Then, walking along the darkened streets, Kayla started looking for the cops. The irony. But just in case they were looking for her—she lived in that fear—she put on her hat and wrapped a scarf around her face, leaving just her eyes exposed.

In this neighbourhood it didn't take long to find cops. The cop car pulled over when she waved. When she saw the one cop's face, it was familiar. He was one of the nice ones. The other was a female cop she didn't recognize.

She sucked in her breath.

"My friend...my friend is...unaccounted for," she said when they rolled down the window. *Unaccounted for* was easier than any of the other possibilities. Of which there were so many.

She explained that outreach workers had already filed a report about Little Zoe and that she had new info: Little Zoe might be with a guy named Nate who had a place by the lake.

When she said the man's name, the cops looked at each other. Just enough. The one murmured something under her breath to the other. They entered the information in, but Kayla had seen the look.

Downtown, the falling snow ate the sounds of the street. Even though it was light out by now, the city was only just waking up, with just a few tire tracks through the snow.

Mama B would be sleeping, but Naomi and Marcel's tent was a place you could always go at this hour. They were always up early, packing up before bylaw came.

She made her way to the alley where their tent would be, her footsteps first in the freshly fallen snow. Outside their tent, their mat was there, WELCOME faintly visible. But there were no noises coming from their tent, which was odd. By now Naomi and Marcel would usually be getting ready to head out and go about their day.

"Naomi," Kayla whispered. There was no response. "Naomi."

She jostled their cart beside the tent so that it would rattle—the closest thing to a doorbell there was on the street. But that was met only by silence.

"Naomi." Just silence.

She reached for the tent's zipper. She pulled it down slowly, just a bit.

Inside, she could see Naomi and Marcel. Instead of being curled together in their comforter, they were sitting, heads slumped over on each other. Sometimes they slept like that, leaning against the lingering heat of a building, together but in their separate journeys.

On this morning, a shared blanket was pulled around their shoulders. But the blanket was too still.

Thursday, 8:00 a.m.

In the cold of Leon, an ambulance came with sirens, tire tracks striping the snow of the alley. Paramedics jumped out. Folks from the street gathered around, coming from wherever they had been sleeping. They watched and hoped but knew. It wasn't the first time.

The street was a place where people were here and then they weren't. People left because they had dreams to follow and elsewheres to get to, the promise of something and somewhere different, a new place to begin again. People left because they had fallen out with someone on the street or had done their dealer wrong and needed to flee. People went into rehab when a space finally became available. People went to work or prison. People left because there was hope of family, of reconciliation, of a second chance. And people left in ambulances, sometimes with the sirens turned off.

Tears stung Kayla's face in the cold. The snow continued to fall in the brittle morning light.

Lit candles, held in glass jars to protect them from the wind, started appearing against the wall of the alley. Someone made a cardboard sign with *RIP—We love you Naomi & Marcel* in permanent marker. Derek brought a poem he wrote, torn from his beloved notebook. Nelson placed a fruit bowl underneath the sign, a find from his rounds of salvaging. Even Teflon came, and lay down a pair of brass knuckles as if in concession for what Naomi had never liked.

"I wish the city had the piano out for the season," Dan-o said, "I'd bring it here and play." He brought his guitar instead, and played into the wind.

Kayla stayed in the alley, sitting on her backpack, staring at where Naomi and Marcel's tent had been. The morning's snow was trampled away with so many footsteps, along with the tire tracks of the ambulance that had come too late.

When was the moment that marked the difference between having a body and being a body? Where was that line between saveable and unsaveable? The line where you realized it was time to save yourself, if you could, before it was too late? What was you? What could and could not be extinguished? Kayla stared at the concrete wall in front of her, with its layers of graffiti, so many swirls and possible words and no clear answers.

Ordinarily, Naomi or Marcel would have given the other the Naloxone shot if the other had gone over the edge and become unresponsive: that's why it was safer always to use together. Kayla knew the principles. Everyone on the street knew. So she was surprised to learn, when the tent was packed up, that there had been no Naloxone kits found in the tent. None at all. Naomi and Marcel always kept a few so they could give one to someone who needed it. But they must have given them all away.

Thursday, 2:00 p.m.

Cerise found Kayla in the alley that afternoon. Kayla had been watching people come and go, paying their respects at the only place there was to mourn. From down the street came Eddie's yells, louder than usual. News of the morning's loss had trickled through the streets as news always did. One by one, people made their way to the alley, leaving what they thought Naomi and Marcel would have liked, or perhaps, as Kayla thought when Dan-o put down a bottle of whiskey with some remaining, what would have meant something to themselves. Marta came by, not leaving anything, but just to be there, and Kayla knew there would soon be two new rows on the blanket she always knitted.

"I can't believe it," Cerise said. But given the losses on the street, both she and Kayla could believe it. They just couldn't believe it happened to people they loved: Naomi who gave out roses to those who needed them or didn't yet know they did, Naomi who believed in community more than policing. Marcel with his dreams of making music, sharing the best fruit he secretly saved for folks on the street. Both of them with the WELCOME mat they always meant. They had been there after those first few nights Kayla had started working the street. They had been there when Little Zoe had her overdose, when Gloria lost her first street daughter, when it was time to crowd into City Pizza for a holiday. When there was a birthday to celebrate, candles lit in the dark of evening. They had been there those nights and many more: nights when the laughter was late and loud, nights when the laughter came easy, and nights when the laughter came hard.

"We need to go," Cerise said. She stiffened when Kayla tried to hug her. "We have to pack up Little Zoe's stuff. Or they're going to throw it all out."

Cerise was right. It was well over forty-eight hours since Little Zoe was last at Hearthstone. Nearly a week. Extensions were extended for someone like her, but this was too long. Her bed needed to become free. The staff had agreed to bend the rules—had gone well beyond them—but could only look away so long.

Kayla felt the collective swell of sadness as soon as they stepped in the door of the shelter. The frequency of death did not lessen its pain; it only underscored that life out here was so fragile.

Kayla and Cerise went past the safe injection area, where people were bent over the table. Kayla's feet felt heavy as she walked past the beds, past the people in their sleeping bags or staring at the ceiling.

Little Zoe's bed was the same. Her purple duvet was pulled up to the satin pillow, alongside her stuffed unicorn and her well-loved platypus, its plush worn. Beside her bed was the locker mirror she used to get ready, along with a picture of a sunny mountain, ripped from a magazine—her view when she wanted to focus on something beyond what was around her. Her gold miniskirt was hanging on the hanger duct-taped to the wall; her flip-flops were under her bed, along with a big plastic bin.

"I'm gonna get a garbage bag," Cerise said. "Gonna store all her things under my bed until she's back."

It was not the first time Little Zoe's possessions would be put into a garbage bag. Kayla recalled how Little Zoe said she had grown up bringing all she owned in one garbage bag as she went from foster home to foster home. She said it was just part of how she had learned how to live from moment to moment, how she had learned to make both friends and impressions fast. She had learned that along with how to keep parts of herself closed off without seeming to, so she had something left when everything had to change again.

They hauled the bin out from under Little Zoe's bed. Inside were dresses, plus a couple of sweaters from the outreach workers. Then there was a fleece onesie, splashed with unicorns, in a children's size. They had seen it on Little Zoe once when she was sick. That must have been an especially impossible day; they usually didn't have the luxury of taking time off.

The smallness of Little Zoe's clothes struck Kayla. Even though Little Zoe was tiny, these clothes seemed far too small for someone who lived so big.

There was her make-up bag, and the Ziploc filled with the nail polish with which Little Zoe painted each of her nails a different colour. There was the sunny yellow her daughter loved the most.

Near the bottom of the bin was a bag with a package of coloured pipe cleaners and a canister of sequins, a glue stick and a box of crayons, unused. There was a bag of plastic beads that, when Kayla looked more closely, were enough to spell out the letters of Little Zoe's firstborn's name.

There was a scrapbook half-filled with banana stickers, which Kayla knew Little Zoe had been collecting since childhood. Apples and bananas were usually available in the Ministry of Children and Family Development offices. Her sticker collection was extensive.

There was Little Zoe's sudoku book. She loved solving the puzzles, finding everything a place.

There was an eggshell collage on construction paper, with her daughter's name written out in a child's hand. Along with, *MOM.*

There was the Christmas card Cerise had given her. Santa, *HO HO HO.* Cerise's handwriting: *For my favourite ho. Love you.*

There was also a picture of a brown-haired girl in pigtails that Kayla recognized as Little Zoe's daughter from that day at the pizza place. If her friend had meant to leave, had time to do so, wouldn't she have brought this photo with her, of all things?

At the very bottom of the bin there was a college course catalogue, one page's corner folded. When Cerise picked it up a piece of paper fell out. A typed letter. Circled on the page in the catalogue was a social work program. And the letter was a conditional acceptance from Okanagan College, with information about funding.

Kayla and Cerise looked at each other. Little Zoe had never said a thing.

Sometimes they had been so focused on survival, on the next day and the next hour and the next minute and the next second, that they hadn't told each other all they dreamed. If there had been time to dream at all.

There was also the jewellery box Nelson had salvaged for her, the one with the ballerina who no longer danced. Nelson had said he could fix it, that she could twirl again. Kayla remembered how Little Zoe had looked when he'd said it—how she had smiled.

I have danced.

And she had: the many days and nights in clubs, wearing her platform heels that lasted long and well despite all she did, climbing poles and forgetting she was being watched. With the lights on her, the crowd dark, it was possible. She'd told Kayla how she would hear the music, sometimes songs that were expected and sometimes entirely different and surprising, sometimes ones that were about going through the motions and some she really felt deep. For those songs she would move not as if the music determined her movements or she determined it, but as if she and the music were making it happen together. *Yes, I've danced.*

Do you want me to fix her? Nelson had asked.

She had looked at the little plastic ballerina in the box—paint chipped, little tutu around her waist, eyes just tiny dots, slightly uneven, a doll ready to spin in a circle—and murmured, *No. She's better dancing in my head.*

Cerise opened the jewellery box, though Kayla didn't think she needed to; she could have just put it under her own bed for safekeeping. Inside the jewellery box were necklaces and bracelets and rings Kayla had seen her friend wear, depending on the outfit and the night. She held up the beaded bracelet Sally had made for Little Zoe, and the necklace from Thursday Man. There was the locket Kayla had never seen her wear, the one Livia had given her on outreach. Inside was a black and white photo of someone else's grandmother, with a wrinkled, apple doll face. Little Zoe had wanted that locket because she hoped one day to give it to her daughter, with a picture of her own. *I'm saving this for something special.*

Something special. Kayla recalled Kori's words.

For all Little Zoe kept, Kayla noticed that the pearl earrings, which Little Zoe now wore on Fridays for Ice Cream Man, were gone. It had been a Friday when they had last seen Little Zoe.

Kayla remembered the way Ice Cream Man had raised his hand at her, the look on his face when he took the earrings back. But how Little Zoe had worn them. She remembered Little Zoe saying that sometimes she and the man stayed at the lake after dark, walking the shore, watching the sunset until the sky became stars.

And there, in the bottom of the jewellery box, where the velvet had started to peel away, was a crumpled piece of paper.

Cerise plucked it out and they saw it was not one but many pieces of different sizes, colours, and textures, crushed together. On them were little designs. Kayla could see dragons and skulls—perhaps possible tattoo ideas someone had drawn for her—and then more pieces of varying intricacy: numbers surrounded by swirls, crossed-out sketches, the curl of an infinity symbol. Kayla recalled the places on Little Zoe's body she'd talked about getting inked: places etched in cigarette burns and places that were still unmarked skin.

Something made Kayla want to rescue these tiny pieces of paper—was it Cerise's casual disregard as she was sifting through her friend's belongings? The fragility of those little scraps? Or that Little Zoe must have created these—or some of them—and they could mean something? Even be a clue? No matter—they didn't deserve to be kept in this box, shoved under Cerise's bed in a garbage bag.

Kayla took them. She would look at them later, alone. For now, she just tucked them in her backpack, gently so as not to ruin them.

Thursday, 5:00 p.m.

"Fuck off!" A man Kayla didn't know had jumped up from his bunk and was waving a knife at Kori, who had finally secured a bed in the shelter. "Go to hell!"

"I'm already in it!" Kori screamed. She grabbed at the blade of the knife. Held it in her hand. She did not let go even after blood started raining down.

"Jesus," Cerise said from where she and Kayla stood by Little Zoe's bed. She and Kayla watched as the Hearthstone staff rushed towards the man, the knife, Kori.

Even before staff reached him, the man threw the knife clattering onto the floor. He sank, crumpling, and then curled himself into a ball. He wailed like a wounded animal, though he had no physical wounds. The painful sound filled the shelter.

Kori was holding her hand, strangely silent. There was blood all over, dripping onto the floor.

"Jesus," Cerise said again, but none of them were surprised.

It was one of those days. People were in grief, and grief could come out in ugly ways.

Even beyond what had happened with the knife, the climate of Hearthstone and on the street was at once sad and electric. Those who were given to yelling yelled more; those who cried cried more; those who used used more.

Many folks were now rushing out the back door of the shelter. They seemed less concerned that the man would rise again from where he lay, holding himself and screaming, and more concerned about being there when the first responders arrived. They could be the police, depending. No one wanted any trouble. And many had seen enough first responders for that day.

Cerise and Kayla shoved Little Zoe's belongings under Cerise's bed.

"I've got to fucking get to work," Cerise said, meaning she needed the relief that work would soon afford. But Kayla saw in her friend's eyes not just her addiction but the same anguish she felt. The deep, horrible feeling of having packed up Little Zoe's things. Of knowing what it might mean.

"Come with me," Cerise pleaded. "Let's get to work. Fuck getting all pretty. Let's just go."

"No," Kayla said. "I'm not going."

She listened to herself say the words—"I'm not going."

A glare flickered across Cerise's face. "Fuck it then. I'm going without you." Without her makeup, wearing just the clothes she already had on, she stormed away.

Kayla sat there a moment. Then she made sure all Little Zoe's things were tucked under Cerise's bed. Beside it, the naked mattress of Little Zoe's bed stared back at her.

She picked up her backpack, with those little crumpled pieces of paper buried inside. Then she left Hearthstone and walked towards the lake, heading there instead of the corner.

Cold cut through her jacket. She bent against the weather. She walked by people gathered, their breath visible in the cold afternoon air. She walked past the alley, past the makeshift memorial, where a tent should have been. Tiny, hard snowflakes pelted her face. The street was quiet with snow.

Kayla was grateful to get to the park. She sat on a bench facing the lake. Nelson sat on another bench, staring out at the dark water. She knew he wouldn't come over. They just stayed there apart but together in the cold.

Then she thought of Little Zoe's letter from the college. Could it be possible that Little Zoe had actually left to start a new life? That she had severed herself from this life the only way she knew how? Completely, in a moment when she finally got the courage?

Kayla knew about severing yourself from where you were.

But perhaps Little Zoe had something to go to, or at least something she was going to try and find. On this day, could Kayla hope for that?

She wanted to take out the little pieces of paper she'd saved, as if they might mean something. Perhaps she just longed to hold something of her friend in her hands. But the time didn't feel right. Not on this day of violence and pain.

She sat for a long time.

When she looked up at the moon, it seemed especially scarred that night.

Thursday, 8:00 p.m.

The buzz of her phone made Kayla jump. She grabbed it quickly.

But it wasn't Little Zoe.

3400 Lakeshore Road.

Then a moment later: *That's Nate's address. Nate Grayson is his name.*

Kayla read Mandy's words and felt a shred of hope. Perhaps she would find Little Zoe working on a long date, or partying at that guy's house, her phone dead or gone. Perhaps Little Zoe would laugh at her and tell her not to have worried so much. Perhaps.

I got an address where Little Zoe might be, Kayla texted Cerise. Kayla figured that given the time she'd spent at the lake, staring at the water, Cerise would have been on a few dates already. Would have then earned enough to score the drugs she needed. The look in her eyes had said she needed it even more today. And if Cerise had gotten what she needed, she might be steadier by now, filled with enough to function but not so much that she was too fucked up. There was always that sweet spot. It was worth trying.

Where are you? Want to go with me? I'll start walking towards the alley. See if I can find you.

She breathed.

See if we can find Little Zoe.

*

"Ketchum got arrested this morning," Mama B was saying as Kayla approached the people clustered around the shelter, not far from the alley where Cerise often went. "They got him this morning when he was at the memorial."

Derek was there, no fishing hat on, and so were Gloria, Sally, and Mel. Mel had Buster on a leash. Kayla stroked Buster's fur.

Jail—Ketchum had been in jail more than enough. And now he couldn't come with her.

Kayla tried to steady her voice. "I heard about where Little Zoe might be, though. I'm going to go check. Cerise in the alley?"

"Yeah," Mama B answered. "She's not doing so great."

"None of us are. Not today."

Kayla headed towards the mouth of they alley, glittering with broken glass. In its darkness, she found Cerise, leaning against the wall, eyes closed.

"Cerise. I got an address where Little Zoe might be."

Cerise was silent except for a little sigh. Her purse and a needle were at her feet. She sank down to the ground, sitting with her knees pulled to her chest.

"I'm going to go find her, and wondered if..." Kayla started, but didn't bother finishing.

Thursday, 8:30 p.m.

Kayla would have to go on her own. If Ketchum had been around, he surely would have offered to join her. No doubt Mel would have, too—she was tough in her own way. But no one had seen her. And Kayla felt only a singular sense of mission, an urgency she could not ignore.

She was just going to Nate's to ask if Little Zoe was there. Or if she had been recently. To hopefully see that she still was. She mapped the address on her phone and set off. Streams of headlights and taillights streaked by as she walked past businesses, gas stations, waterfront restaurants, motels, condos, beaches, then houses with lake views and backyard docks. As the numbers grew closer to the address for which she was looking, her breath quickened.

Then, eventually, she saw it. The house was modern, angular, and huge. The blinds on the windows were pulled, just a few rectangles of light behind. Beyond the house, she could see the lake and a dock, a boat covered for winter. There was a long driveway leading from the road, heading to a triple garage, and surrounding the property, a spiked metal fence, taller than she was, with a gate. The gate was open.

If Little Zoe was staying here, it certainly would have been a lucrative place to work.

Kayla sucked in her breath and started walking, both her footsteps and her heart rate fast. She could hear no music. There was no party going on. At least not of that sort.

She climbed the curved steps leading up from the walkway and rang the doorbell. Waited.

Nothing. No footsteps, no voices. Just nothing.

She rang again.

And then she heard someone coming, pause at the door to look out at her, turn the lock. A man opened it, slowly and just halfway. He didn't say anything. Just stared at her. He was clean shaven with short hair. He had the eyes of someone who was using.

He looked at her for a moment. Then his lips curled with a hint of a smile. "Can I help you?"

"I'm wondering if my friend is here. Little Zoe."

The man was quiet for a moment, as if taking her in. "No. No one is here but me."

"Was she here though? A friend said she was here."

"Haven't see her." But there was something in his eyes. There was definitely something.

"But they said she was here. I just need to know where she is."

"She's not here." Then more than a hint of a smile. He opened the door wider. "But you are. You could be."

Friday, 7:00 a.m.

Kayla paced the city streets as they quieted, slept, and started to come to life again. She just kept staring at that ever-pinkening sky, hoping the wrenching in her gut was wrong.

She had fled the man's house as quickly as she came, realizing that whatever had happened there—if anything had happened—could also happen to her. And she sensed, in a way that she could not explain but felt, that if Little Zoe had been there at all, she was not there any longer.

And her fear was not contained to just this one man. He had given her a terrible feeling, but there were others, too. What about Ice Cream Man with his surprisingly stern grip? That farm north of Vernon? Or someone else who haunted—and perhaps hunted—downtown?

Kayla walked and walked.

And then she saw Little Zoe's face.

Staring out from a poster duct-taped to the pole of a streetlight: those eyes, that smile. Below the photo were a few details about her friend, her weight and height and tattoos. There was contact info for the outreach organization, in case anyone with information preferred not to talk to police.

Below that, MISSING.

Missing. She really was.

Missing.

Gone? She didn't want to think it. But missing, yes.

No matter how Kayla could rationalize or justify, make excuses or conjure ideas or feel feelings, that much was true.

And Kayla missed her, fiercely.

Kayla stared into her friend's face. Those eyes that could open wounds or heal them.

Kayla fished in her jacket for her phone. Wanting to finally have a picture of her friend, she held her phone front of her. She zoomed in, past MISSING, and focused just on that smile with the gap where her tooth was pulled, and those eyes that crinkled into crescent moons, those eyes that knew how to bring kindness because some kindness was needed in this world, those eyes that had seen so much but still, somehow, knew how to see joy and possibility.

Kayla remembered that first morning on the bench in the park, when she'd first met Little Zoe, saying the she knew of a place where it was alright to be.

She remembered that day on the beach, when she was new to town and she and Little Zoe had their first real talk, how Little Zoe's words felt so right, the way she said them.

She remembered that evening on Dilworth Mountain, sitting together among the wildflowers, overlooking the city, those distant lights, how Little Zoe had known Kayla needed to see something different.

She remembered what Little Zoe always said: know when it's time to go.

She remembered Little Zoe floating in the water, laughing and free, always trying to feel the freest she could feel.

I hope, wherever you are and whatever you are doing, that you feel that freedom.

Kayla took the picture. Then she lowered her phone.

She took a moment. A long moment.

Then she had to be in the present.

She felt the cold wind from the lake on her face and knew what she had to do.

Livia, she texted. *I need you to talk to the cops.*

Spring

February's chill gave way to March's changeability and then to April's promising warmth. Days lengthened, spring thawed, lingering snow disappeared, tourists trickled into downtown, the shelter kept serving its chili and its soup. Kori kept selling her findings, Gloria kept collecting her medicines, Ketchum kept spending days in jail, Nelson kept salvaging treasures. Okanagan sunflowers sprouted and orchards leafed out and dandelions bloomed.

And still nothing of Little Zoe.

Of course, Livia kept Kayla updated on Little Zoe's file. Livia and Wanjiru kept checking in with the police, demanding updates and progress, or at least ongoing effort. Livia would tell Kayla about it when they went to Livia's and cooked together, sometimes with Wanjiru. But there were no real updates to tell.

Kayla had heard lots at first—everyone had ideas of what had happened or where Little Zoe had gone—but then it was almost as if some people accepted her absence. That loss was just a part of their lives and there was nothing they could do.

Kayla could not accept it.

Unaccounted for. Kayla remembered her words to the police. *My friend is unaccounted for.*

Unaccounted for. Did that mean not counting or the opposite of not counting?

Her worries echoed amidst all she could not know.

Then, one day, she knew at least one thing.

I have something I want to show you, Livia had texted.

They met in City Park.

"I found something in the paper," Livia said. She unfolded piece of newsprint from her purse and started to read aloud.

"We are deeply sorry to announce the sudden passing of our son, Nathan (Nate) Grayson, after a battle with addiction and a tragic overdose..."

"The man at the house on Lakeshore."

They looked at each other, many thoughts between them.

But perhaps it didn't mean much more than another tragic casualty in the pandemic that had killed more people in the province than the other pandemic that everyone spoke about. Another needless loss, another family to grieve, another life cut short.

Another story that would never finish.

Perhaps.

Late April

And then, on a day not long after, Kayla found something else.

It was a bright blue day. Boats played across the lake. Though the water was cold, swimmers swam, desperate for the beach and stoic in the way Canadians were this time of year. Shirtless guys threw around a frisbee. Some kids were on an inflatable Ogopogo, splashing. People lounged with beach umbrellas and towels, smearing optimistic sunscreen on their backs.

Kayla had been walking, barefoot in the cold water, when she saw it. There among the pebbles, in the dark sand where the water lapped the shore, Kayla found a fingernail.

A nail with sunny yellow polish. Little Zoe's daughter's favourite colour.

It could have been so casually lost. Or it could have belonged to anyone. It could have meant anything, or nothing at all. Just something small. Perhaps a coincidence rather than a clue. Or perhaps part of a much larger story.

But on that clement spring day, with time passing and the missing posters becoming sun-bleached, and no solid leads to believe in beyond what was increasingly in her heart, Kayla just stared out at the dark water.

She wished she knew what was true, but the only truth was the depth of the lake and the murk down there, the shafts of sunlight that reach down and down until they cannot reach any further.

Early May

"She did *what?*"

Kayla was staring down Leon, standing outside the shelter and looking all the way towards the park and the lake. The sidewalks were cleared of any tents. The usual people weren't there.

"Kori fucking ratted on us," Mama B was saying bitterly. "Told bylaw that I had that heater. That Gloria had a bed. All Gloria wanted was somewhere to rest her old bones. Be comfortable. All I wanted was to stay warm."

"Why'd she tell on us all?"

Mama B just shrugged. "Maybe they had something on her she wanted cleared? So maybe she told on us so they'd look away?"

Kayla had come from sleeping under *t'st'siɬp* to find Mama B standing alone on her usual stretch of sidewalk, with nothing and no one else in sight.

"Got us while we were just starting our day," she told Kayla, recounting how bylaw had pulled up, not only in their marked SUVs, but with a big truck, too. Without warning they'd flooded the streets, yelling at the tents, barking orders and unzipping the doors, forcing people from their shelters, invading, confiscating, hurling belongings into trucks not caring at breakage. They threatened arrest for anyone who tried to stop them or refused.

Kayla shook her head solemnly, staring at the empty streets. Of course they weren't empty: there were people and cars and the usual business of the day. But their friends had scattered.

"Bylaw said our camp was a fire hazard. That's always their excuse to clear us out. Didn't give us time to pack up properly. Just started taking all our stuff. Telling us to move along. Destroying what little we had."

"Why now? We've been here all winter."

"Had to get the city all shiny before May 24 weekend, before the tourists come."

Kayla remembered how Naomi had resisted.

"We cleared out pretty fast, but we'll find each other again," Mama B consoled. "And if we know anything, we know how to start from scratch."

The MISSING posters were still wrapped around streetlights. The police kept their file open. Livia still walked the city some nights after outreach, looking.

A handmade sign reading—COME IN NOW—CLOSING SOON—was in the window of the pub with the sign lit only with the letter E. The new condos on Leon were soon to be built. Bylaw scoured downtown more than ever. People on the street weren't sure where they would go. New shelters would be opened, the City assured. And of course there would be new pubs. But the communities who lived there feared losing the places and people they knew. Scattered as they were, they still gathered sometimes, looked out for one another.

Then one day, with the mountains greening and clouds unfurling above, Nelson came up to Kayla in the park.

"I found something."

She felt her heart race and gut plummet.

He rummaged in his pack, then held out his hand. And there was an old Polaroid camera. "It was broken, but I fixed it."

She stared at the relic.

"I had one once," he told her. "It's the kind that lets you give people pictures. The image just comes out. See here? At first the picture comes out opaque. But then it becomes clearer."

He told her of the Polaroid camera he'd had overseas. While at war, all he did was destroy and take, but this sort of camera had allowed him to give.

Then he handed it to her. It was heavy in her hands, but she was grateful.

And so Kayla started to take pictures with that camera, sometimes on walks with Livia, sometimes on her own—pictures of what needed to be remembered, what needed to be celebrated, what needed to be seen with new eyes. Sharing her pictures to her friends, she hoped to bring brightness on days when they might need it, like Naomi had with her roses or Marcel with his fruit.

Kayla got a picture of Dan-o at the piano under the canopy of trees, playing the songs he had shared with so many and playing the songs he would continue to share for all who would listen.

She got one of Mama B on her usual stretch of sidewalk, though it wasn't where she slept anymore. Still ready to hug or bandage or lend an ear, she was no longer sleeping on the street, had gotten into community housing. She now had a one-room place with a kitchenette and bathroom—no bathtub, as she longed for—but she had a shower of her own. Her faucet dripped, and she was grateful to have a faucet to drip. She showed Kayla pictures on her phone: a simple room with a bed, milk crates holding her clothes, and a lamp that Nelson had salvaged.

But in her own place she was so lonely, Mama B said. You couldn't have visitors in your apartment. That was to prevent drug dealing, they said. Away from her street family, in her little room of one, it felt like an extension of prison, where she had spent enough time. She knew she should be happy, but she found she couldn't sleep without the sounds of the street, the voices of her friends. And she missed the stars. So Alexa had stolen stars for her, the kind that glow in the dark once stuck to the ceiling. Mel and Sally, who had inherited Naomi and Marcel's tent, suggested she set up her tent in her room to make it feel more like home. So Mama B did, and slept in there, waiting for the day when more folks could get into housing and they could be together again.

"Oh, there's gonna be a day when we all have roofs," she said. "Imagine what we can do then." Then she sidled up to Kayla: "But sometimes I still feel most at home out with the stars."

Kayla took a picture of Gloria, Sally, and a new street daughter, Laurie, who collected medicines and drank morning tea together. Gloria would be there for them and for any new children who came: there with blankets and advice and stories, teaching them how to bead and how to survive beyond what they had already lived through. And she would ask them *c'kin aspuʔus*?

To her care and generosity, Sally learned to reply, *limt ispuʔus. My heart is full with happiness.*

And Sally's heart was full these days. Kayla got a picture of Mel and Sally, both flecked with a rainbow of paint from transforming bikes in the park. They were in front of their tent, arms around each other, with the welcome mat they had inherited from Naomi and Marcel. It was a mat they put out every night and meant. Buster was at their feet, wagging.

Kayla took a photo of Cerise staring down Leon Avenue as if she owned it. And these days, there was a new strength in her step. Beyond the work she did from their corner—it would always be their corner—these days she had also connected with a group of sex workers online. They were committed to working towards decriminalization and more rights, which would mean more safety for workers. Cerise had started talking about better working conditions more and more, while using drugs less and less. *Together, we can have a voice,* Kayla heard her say more than once. *We've survived by not putting up with shit, and we're not putting up with the shit that keeps us down any more.* There was a new gleam in her eye.

Lily was still on the corner too. But Kayla didn't take a picture of her there. She got one of her in the park, with the soccer ball she had reclaimed. She would bring it to the park to kick around with friends. She started to make new friends, too.

Kayla also got a picture of Marta with her cart of treasures, and her knitted Always blanket with the zigzag rows that would not stop. Rows honouring Naomi and Marcel were there. She had new yarn, a gift from Wanjiru, who brought skeins of wool along with her hot meals. Wanjiru also brought her nursing students, exposing them to the realities of the street so that they, too, could provide care that mattered. Marta, like the rest, appreciated that, but was especially glad to have the wool: there would be more hats and mittens to knit, just as there would be more rows on her Always blanket.

Kayla got a picture of Derek with his notebook, fishing hat on, making his vivid world real as he wrote it, spinning folks into a tale when they felt invisible and needed to be seen, creating worlds that needed to be created.

He was not the only one creating, though. Kayla got a picture of Tyler standing proudly with a carving he made with the man in the woods: a beaver, like the one he had seen making a dam in the river, a home. He was going to the woods more often those days. Some said he had met a girl.

Kayla got one of Alexa in her in her special necklace and her favourite magenta dress, the one she had designed and sewn herself. She had plans for more. As soon as she could get a place, she was getting a sewing machine of her own.

Teflon was there, too, and Kayla got one of her in her many rings. Teflon had been directing traffic for drivers who didn't know Leon was a one-way street at points. Despite all she got up to, she'd been helping those who didn't know. Kayla was glad to have a picture of that side of Teflon too, because there was one.

She got one of Kori. These days Kori's belly was swollen as if she were pregnant, though she said she was not. Mama B said it was liver failure. Kori had lost a few more teeth. Kayla had learned by now some people faded away in increments and some people faded fast.

She got one of Eddie on a day good enough that he actually asked for a picture. He had looked right at the camera. *I'm telling you,* he said, but then he smiled, and left it at that. Most days and nights you could find him storming up and down Leon, with headphones on, trying to drown out the voices. Dogs continued to have messages for him. And of course people had messages as well—both people heard by others and those who were silent for the rest. *Listen!* he would yell some days, his voice echoing down the street. *Won't anyone fucking listen?*

Kayla didn't get a picture of Jason. He was in jail. But if he had been there, Kayla would have gotten a picture of him with his arm around Blaze, who was now being looked after by Mel and Sally. Blaze and Buster often curled together in their sleep.

Nelson didn't want his picture taken. One day, Kayla saw him from a distance in the park, staring out at the lake, and the way the light shone on his ancient-seeming features and grizzled beard seemed so perfect. But she kept walking, camera down. And he kept finding and giving treasures. Fixing what he could fix. Giving what he could give. Sometimes, though it didn't always look it from the outside, he gave what was needed most.

She also, of course, didn't have the chance to take a picture of Little Zoe. So Kayla took a picture of their street corner. Empty. Yet not empty. Kayla didn't stop listening to the streets for Little Zoe's footsteps, the clicking of her heels.

Some nights, walking those streets, at once familiar but ever-changing, Kayla even thought she could smell a trace of her friend's perfume, floating in the air.

She gave many photographs away but also kept some for herself: some of her friends and some she was just trying out, experimenting to see what could happen, what she was capable of doing. And some magic happened beyond her control or intention. Kayla saw how hues of blue emerged when temperatures were cooler, and how in certain light, the edges were dark and blurry, just the centre in real focus, but that you could tell there was more beyond.

Sometimes Livia would come with her. Livia didn't take pictures herself on those walks, bringing her camera along but never raising it. She just walked with Kayla, pausing when Kayla stopped to take a photo. She seemed hesitant to take pictures of her own, yet she enjoyed seeing Kayla's photos: the faces of friends, a deep yellow sunflower after it burst through hard spring ground.

One day after wandering down Leon and the alleys, they ended up at the Safeway parking lot where Livia always parked her car.

"This. I want to take a picture of this," Livia said suddenly, pointing to the brick wall of Safeway, the view at which she had stared so many times, when she sat in her car, parked and drinking. "I want to remind myself that I was there. So many evenings, staring at that wall."

She raised her camera, steadied her hands, took a picture.

"It's a start," were her words when they finally came.

That was when Kayla decided to bring her up to Dilworth Mountain, just as Little Zoe had done for her. To see something different when difference is what you needed to see.

Kayla directed her up the winding roads. After Livia parked her car, they walked past the park with its swing set, and into the meadow surrounded by cottonwoods and pine. On that morning the cottonwoods were so sweet, just beginning to bloom.

There, before them, stretched a sea of Okanagan sunflowers. Golden flowers were everywhere, nodding in the wind. Some were in full flower and some were on the verge. Others remained curled close to the earth, barely seen.

Livia was quiet for a moment.

And then she raised her camera.

As she heard the click, Kayla realized she had given her friend a gift. And she was glad she had been able to give it. From her street family, her family, she had learned how much it meant to give what you were capable of giving.

For a long time, they stood there, looking.

Beyond them, the field of flowers breathed.

Mid-May

Are you out there?

Kayla stared at the cracked screen of her phone at Demi Ray's words. They had come out of the blue.

How did you get my number? Kayla asked, remembering how careful she had tried to be once she'd fled across the country. She'd switched her number, along with nearly everything else. But then she remembered texting Demi Ray from out here, one night in a desperate need to reach out. She could barely remember that night—times on the street could do that. She remembered only the intensity.

Oh—of course you have it. And I'm very glad.

It wasn't that Kayla hadn't thought of Demi Ray, but given what she had been up to herself, she hadn't kept in touch. It had been part pride, part fear, part the grit and grind of day-to-day survival. And it was also because she had found real friends out west, a community who were with her day in and day out. It didn't mean those times with Demi Ray and Sebastian hadn't mattered, or that what she and Demi Ray had shared was any less. And she respected that Demi Ray was busy, no doubt continuing with her successes, or giving it all she had to get there, riding countless horses, putting in the work.

I'm so glad to hear from you. How are you these days?

Demi Ray, who tended to keep her messages brief—though would hopefully share long stories someday—wrote back in time. Kayla hadn't expected a response right away; she knew Demi Ray spent most of her days on a horse.

So much to tell you, her message came at last. *So much has happened. Don't really know where to begin. And some's not worth telling. I could spend forever in all the updates and details. And haha it all changes by the day and sometimes I don't know myself! But here's a bit of what I'm up to...*

Demi Ray didn't dwell on the long hours—she'd grown and raised herself up knowing hard work—but delved into the horses, the unique training solutions and ideas she was developing for each: who was developing a great hind leg or extensions, the patience and rewards of the canter pirouette with a favourite mare. *But many are special in their own ways, you know that*—and Kayla did know that, appreciated that Demi Ray could still speak in as if in shorthand to her, trusting she would understand.

Well not all of them haha. Some horses don't have it. And some are decent but just go through their days and do their jobs. But a few...

Demi Ray was staying down south for now, soaking it all in. The victories were continuing—not always in the form of ribbons and awards, but nonetheless being recognized as the top rider Kayla knew she was. And parts of her were surely the same. No doubt she still gave herself Banamine from the vet supplies when she was hurt, would probably still file her own teeth if she had to.

So Kayla, what are you up to?

Kayla stared at the screen.

I have stories too, she started, but was unsure of how much she should tell. How much she could tell. What was even possible to tell. And perhaps time and distance, and so much more, meant some stories didn't need to be told. Perhaps she and Demi Ray could just pick up again, respecting silences, understanding anyway. But from the sounds of it, from the rhythms of their daily lives, that would be a long time away. But it felt alright, just knowing her friend was there.

And I've been thinking I might try to..., Kayla began.

Late May

The wind off the lake was fresh. As she sat on the rocky beach, the emergent sun felt warm on Kayla's back. And perhaps it was that hope of warmth, or just time—perhaps it was just time—but Kayla felt ready to reach into her backpack for the crumpled pieces of paper she had found in Little Zoe's jewellery box.

After tucking these pieces away when she'd been in the shelter with Cerise, she had taken them back out only once—not to look at them, but to wrap them in Little Zoe's hoodie, keep them safe, and until now, there they had stayed.

She felt compelled see what Little Zoe had left. But then she stopped herself. No, not left: to say she'd left them meant she was gone. And that she had intended to leave these pieces, for them to be found. No, all that could really be said was that Kayla had found these pieces—and what they were, beyond scribbles and designs and marks and musings, was uncertain. So, not left. And gone: was her beloved friend really gone?

She unfolded the first piece gently, as if sacred. She caught glimpses: some were new and striking, whereas others seemed older, something that wouldn't suit her friend anymore.

And then she came across one with only four words on the page: *and here I go.*

And here I go.

It was just words. Maybe just a few words scribbled, something she was trying out. Or could they mean a new life, new horizons? Or was it something like "here I go again"? Or—Kayla felt unstoppable tears welling up with realization of the words' potential—had it been a final goodbye? Had Little Zoe taken herself away for good?

Kayla felt anger then, so much anger, anger that someone she loved so much could have taken themselves away, left her life. *Left.*

For a long time, she stared out at the lake, feeling too much to feel.

But then she realized, watching those waves rise and fall, rise and fall: not left. Not left at all.

Holding those pieces of paper, those words, Kayla at once brimmed with sadness and happiness—a nostalgia for what was lost, and, inexplicably, the feeling that something deeply special was found.

She closed her eyes.

No matter if you've gone, where you've gone, I love you always.

And in that silent speaking, she realized.

She had this. This ability to speak, to love, despite.

In her friend's absence was actually a presence. A presence and a gift.

Little Zoe had given her a way of seeing, a way of being in this world, even when Little Zoe herself—in that body, with those eyes—was elsewhere. And with that gift—*beyond* that gift—was something Kayla realized she had already started to cultivate within herself.

Little Zoe, she said, wanting to share her realization, but even her friend's name didn't seem big enough.

So just:

Thank you.

But what she felt was beyond words.

The End of May

Kayla said it one day to herself, quietly, while under *t'st'siɬp* in the park, sunlight streaming through the branches of the spruce.

"I'm beginning."

Ever since Little Zoe disappeared—and before that, if she thought about it—Kayla had thought about changing her life. With each passing night and each new day, worried for Little Zoe and worried for herself—the times in Hope she didn't want to recall, how she'd almost put that needle into herself again, how she could have lost all she had—she had seen what could happen, what roads she could go down. But more than being ruled by fear, she had seen the possibility of what could come next—and that, for once, she could determine what came next. Or, if she could not determine it, she could at least pick up the reins, aim for something better, ride with whatever came. She had seen she could do more than just endure and go on despite. She could live.

"I'm beginning something new. I'm beginning." She raised her voice a little louder.

She said it again, even louder, to *t'st'siɬp*, to the birds who shared the tree. Having said those words, the gold of the sunset meant something new, let her know that beginnings could start any time, in their own way.

By then she had been working the streets less and less. Unexpectedly, stopping that work felt like a gap opening up. Not a wound, but a gap, something she was missing. She was used to the feeling of being wanted. She was used to earning money, and being in control of how she earned it—in control of something in a world in which she had controlled so little. And she missed how some of the clients had seen her—or had appreciated what she could be to them. The sweet, big guy who just wanted someone to hold him. The acne-stippled teen with his relief. The woman who said, *You let me discover who I really am.* The appreciative look on Thursday Man's face when they talked. There were things she would miss about this work.

Kayla had become Thursday Man's replacement for Little Zoe, and he cried for her one day.

She can't just go like that.

Kayla had agreed. *She can't just go.*

But she had.

And, as Kayla knew in her heart, she also hadn't. Not at all. She was everywhere.

Cerise had lots to say about Kayla stopping work.

"I can't believe you'd do this to me. We're fucking sisters. We've got each other's backs. We *need* each other's backs. We need *each other*."

"You'll still have me," Kayla assured her. "We've been through too much together."

"What are you going to do?"

"I have an idea." But some ideas were just too sacred to speak out loud.

Yet she had said it to herself. Under the branches of her beloved *t'st'siɬp,* with the wind and the birds to hear her. She had said the words and the world around her listened. And so had she.

Also the End of May

Livia had something she was going to try too.

She had vowed to stop drinking.

By then, Livia was on new medication. Though early days yet, it was giving her and her family hope. She didn't know if it was working or just a hopeful placebo, but she would take it either way. At least for now. It was something. And if this medication didn't work, they would try another—but nothing that would numb her, hollow her out, remove the possibility of seeing the beauty in things. She longed for a balance. Could a balance, or something close, be possible? And as she began to feel hope, she felt she was ready to try to stop drinking.

Livia and her family were getting ready to move into the new house they were building, the one in which Kayla had slept once, a new house where there would be no liquor cupboard, no bottles hidden in the pantry. The fridge there would be filled with iced tea rather than wine; hot tea would be there for the cold days. Livia already knew she would take the long way to drop Cara off at preschool, refusing to walk past the liquor store where she had gone so many mornings.

"Are you sure you want to live in the same neighbourhood?" Tom had asked. "We could move further away if..."

"I'll see," Livia said. But no matter where she was, she was solid in her resolve not to drink. It didn't mean she didn't want it, some days. But she wanted to live without it more. And what she really wanted was the beautiful feeling.

She had kept a mickey in the back of her car, under a pile of clothes for outreach, just in case. Then, one day, downtown, the day after Kayla had taken her to Dilworth Mountain and she had taken that first photograph in so long, she had thrown the bottle away. And each day of not drinking, for her, became easier to do. Day by day. Until she craved *that.*

Even after the physical cravings waned—she had gone for long walks many nights as they did, sometimes with Tom, sometimes with Wanjiru, sometimes with Kayla—her thinking had to change. She said that stopping drinking was more than a physical act; it was a way of seeing the world anew. When she told Kayla that, Kayla said it sounded like after her injury, learning to walk again.

And she was doing it. With it came an increased clarity and vitality, as though she were tapping into a brightness she thought she had lost. What she had been chasing in glimmers was, ironically, coming back to her.

She and Cara planted seeds in pots that lined the window sill, sunflowers that promised to grow high when they would plant them at their new house. Together they watched the tiny green shoots emerge, curled in on themselves at first, waiting. Then they watched for them to unfurl.

Livia and Cara had also taken up making pottery, out of a studio in a neighbour's basement. They hand-built with clay, making a dog and an owl. They also used the potter's wheel, which was harder than it looked. You could be making a perfectly good bowl when it could go flying, sent by the force of the wheel. But then you could start again.

Would those times of darkness always be there? And if they weren't there, did that mean the brightness was less intense? If not her companion every moment, perhaps those darknesses would still have a presence, in what they had been, or could possibly be again. Perhaps. But perhaps they were not as dark. Could they too evolve? Was that balance she longed for possible? Something not all encompassing, so she could function in daily life, but which would still allow her to experience the possibility of that brightness?

To try, to see what she could see, to see if she could reach for that brightness, she dared herself to take more pictures.

She took one of Tom and Cara, just a small moment, neither of them looking at the camera. They were getting ready to ride their bikes. Cara's face was full of pride. She was going to ride her big-kid bike, with her training wheels there just in case.

Livia had taken the picture while on a bike of her own. They were all going riding together. Gone were the days she listened for the door to close behind them so she could sneak to the liquor cupboard or the pantry. No, she was right there with them, and she was there.

She showed that picture to Kayla. They had taken Cara to the park together, were watching her playing on the slide and then the swings, pumping and soaring high.

"There's something real there," Kayla said, looking at the picture. "Keep going."

Then Livia dared herself to take more photographs: first a few fallen leaves, closeups of flowers, their fragile petals and golden centres. And more of Cara and Tom.

"It's like I'm literally seeing through a new lens," she told Kayla one day, voice quavering. "I don't doubt that the darkness is out there—but the brightness is coming back. It feels different somehow, but it's here somewhere."

Kayla saw her friend's eyes travel, somewhere far away, just a flicker.

"Mom—look!" came Cara's voice, and she came over to them, holding a leaf with a tiny snail, swirled and beautiful.

"And I feel like for the first time in a long time, I'm getting myself back. I'm *here*."

The Last Day of May

Kayla sat at the lake, where she had felt Little Zoe's absence and presence radiating that day she held those pieces of paper in her hands. The blue of the sky was strong. Sun was on the water.

This time when she took those pieces out—gently, lovingly—she knew what she had to do.

These pieces of paper, these glimpses—what Kayla had so desperately hoped to hold in her own hands, as if such an answer could be easy—Little Zoe may have left them. But she had left far more.

Kayla didn't have any more answers; she had only more questions. And she was beginning to realize that such questions were likely never going to stop. Was *that* the only constant she could hold onto?

Even if Little Zoe had left this life, was gone what she was? Or just changed, the way a cloud turns into rain, how rain and soil and sun together enable a flower to grow?

Feeling not her friend's absence, but presence, she soaked in that moment by the water, seeing how the sunlight caught on each wave for just a glimmer of a moment and then moved on. Not because it wasn't there. It would always be there.

Always.

Then she placed the little pieces of paper at the shore.

I hope you find that freedom.

The Last Night of May

Those on the street were having a party.

Like anything on the street, that unexpected celebration happened right there in the moment, because that moment was what they had.

It started because Kayla told Mama B what she planned to do—saying it quietly at first—and Mama B had been too excited to keep the news to herself.

"I'm not sure if that place will say yes," Kayla told her. "But I'm going to check. To see if they need any help around there."

"They'll say yes. And if they don't, someone else will. So we need to have a goodbye party."

"It's not goodbye. Even if I end up getting work. I'd be back. I'll be back."

"Once you're family, you're family for life."

"You've got us," Gloria added, standing beside her. "No matter what you've got or don't got, you've got us."

They had gathered in the under the trees at the piano, because Dan-o wanted to play. The evening was gold and warm.

Derek had come to the impromptu party, with his new notebook he was glad to have. Kayla had been there the day he bought it at Mosaic Books, counting out all the change he had. Sally came with both Mel and Gloria, who had also brought Laurie, the girl new to town, from a reserve up past 100 Mile House. Alexa was there with her favourite dress on, radiant, and Lily was taking pictures with her phone. Marta was there with her cart and her knitting. Even Nelson came over from his bench by the lake. And of course Buster was there, going from person to person, his tail wagging extra strong.

Mel had brought sushi, Cerise curry. If Naomi and Marcel could have been there, they would have brought fresh-picked fruit. And maybe roses. Someone did bring strawberries from the bungalow that grew the communal garden on Leon, from the house with the tap that provided water on those sweltering summer days. On that last evening the strawberries tasted especially good.

Mama B had brought cupcakes from Safeway. They were iced in periwinkle, Kayla's favourite colour: the colour of the first light of morning, a colour with the potential for anything.

"Got these done special," Mama B was saying. "Real special."

As everyone started to gather, trickling over as news of the party spread through the streets, they talked and told stories of the day, of the night before, of themselves, of what could possibly happen next.

The sky was ever-changing, no moment the same, no light the same, unfolding. Deep violet and then stars. So many stars.

Nelson came over to Kayla, holding something in his worn hands. A little metal box.

"The lid was rusted shut, but it opens now," he told her. "I thought you could use it to keep your pictures safe."

He put it in her hands. She tried it. It stuck a bit, as it was rusty, but then it opened. Inside, there was a space big enough for the pictures she had been taking and would continue to create.

"Thank you." She looked into his eyes. He held her gaze, and then away.

Dan-o's song, which must have started already, continued.

Then Lily was running from person to person, holding a ball. "Come on, guys! Let's play!"

She began bouncing the ball on her knee, then kicked it to Sally. Sally made contact powerfully and Derek ran towards to where it soared, punted, his notebook still in hand. Soon others joined in too.

Kayla had never been one for team sports, but this felt different. She had done lots—was doing lots—that she hadn't expected to do.

They played. She played and played until she was breathless, in a good way.

Then, walking across the park, was Ketchum.

Though he mostly stayed in the woods these days, Ketchum was enjoying being out of jail, at least the one he had been put in for misdemeanors. His thoughts remained haunted after what he had done on the killing floor, haunted after the losses he had not been able to stop. Many days he had wondered who he was as he looked at his hands. But those calloused hands had not just taken so much, had so much pass through them. They'd also built and given so many much-needed hugs, protection, love. And those hands, those arms, had yet more to give.

"Ketchum," she called, her throat growing tight.

But then she had an idea.

"Can you get a picture of us?" she asked Lily.

He nodded and came over, quiet too.

And so Lily took a picture of the two of them, arms around each other: dear friends, or even a dad and a daughter. But not all family, not all love, has such definable names.

Kayla had Lily take two pictures, so Kayla and Ketchum would each have one to keep. Ketchum could now have a picture of family who wanted him in their life for always.

"I've made you a promise before, and I've kept it," she said. "And now I need you to make one."

He looked at her.

"Promise me we'll always keep in touch, no matter where we are or how much time passes. But promise me we'll be there for each other. However we can."

On that night Dan-o's fingers glided across the keys, full of grace and life. In his music he told stories, he gave apologies, he went places for which he had no words. Everyone gathered around him, and he played. Although the piano was not in perfect tune, Dan-o dove right into song, unafraid to change the tune or melody, not waiting for a single, true sound. Or perhaps, in the playing, he found the closest thing to a truth there was. Kayla had often longed for a single, true sound. Now she just listened.

Of Little Zoe, some folks spun suspicions until they became their certainties, from speculations of her grisly death to proclamations of her new start, clean and far away, sometimes with her daughters. Others moved her on from their thoughts, their own lives chaos enough to face as they lived day to day, moment to moment, surviving every way they could.

But on that night Kayla also took more photographs for the friend she would always miss.

"You're taking some for Little Zoe?" Cerise asked when Kayla lingered a bit too long on one. Cerise must have detected something in her face.

"Leave them with me. I'll make sure she gets them soon as she's back." Their ideas about what had happened differed. "And I know you might get this new life, so you might not come back right away, but I'll make sure she gets them...if..."

No, there were no clear answers, no single, true sound.

All Kayla knew was that the glass in the alleyway still glittered, the cracks snaking the walls still watched, the sidewalk still held its stories, and the lake—for all its dark, all its sunlight, and all its waves—still kept its secrets.

But on that night Kayla was saying goodbye—*not really goodbye, not goodbye at all*—to her friends, she was not the only one giving. They all had something to share. Whether curry or whiskey or advice or an ear or a story, they shared. And as the talk and the stories began—stories that started before they were said out loud and stories that would last long after the telling grew quiet—Sally started breathing fire.

Breathing fire was something she had learned on the reserve. She rinsed her mouth with gasoline, then blew against a lighter. They all watched as Sally, who had always been so quiet, breathed fire into the night.

"Here's to doing what we can do," Gloria proclaimed, raising her mug of tea.

Mama B raised a cupcake. "To doing what you can do."

Then Dan-o continued his song.

Before he did, from somewhere in the rustle of the branches or in the wind coming off the lake, Kayla thought that maybe, just maybe, she could hear Little Zoe's laugh.

The stars had been bright in the spaces between the trees, the moon on the lake like glitter.

The Earliest Hours of June

Kayla's footsteps crunched on the gravel roadside as she walked through the windy darkness. Silhouettes of trees flanked the roadside, black against an inky sky bright with stars. Her leg and hip were sore, but she kept walking along that lakeshore road.

It was last summer, on a night just as warm, with the sound of crickets and frogs in the gullies, that she had walked down another gravel shoulder of a road not so different to this, back in Ontario. There had been the distant bark of a dog, the brakes of a truck in the distance. On that night, those had been the only sounds after she left the stirrings of the horses in their stalls, the sound of her own footsteps through the darkened barn. That door closing behind her.

That night she had walked up the driveway, moving as fast as she could go. She had her backpack with her then, just as now. And she had herself.

On that night last summer, she had left a man in her apartment, breathing but damaged, just as he had damaged her.

But she had not let herself be destroyed. She had been changed but not destroyed.

She had walked with the moon as her witness.

Now, almost a year later, here in Kelowna, she walked in the company of the moon again. But it was a different moon.

She looked up at the stars, stars which were memories of what had been there once. She recalled what Livia had said about a photograph she had tried to take of the galaxies: the stars they saw were long gone, but their presence was visible because of how long it took for light to travel. What they looked at were absent suns, something that had once been. This meant, then, that there were new stars out there, ones that they could not yet see.

In the rusted metal box Nelson had given her, buried in the heart of her backpack, she had four photographs.

One was of all her friends by the wall with the mural with words, *kʷu mrímstn. We are medicine.* Painted on the side of the shelter, there stood, not lay, that art. In vibrant colours, there were grandmother spirits who looked over a group of women, who in turn watched over the land, the rivers with their salmon, and, since the mural was along Leon, the entire street. Despite being behind a chain-link fence, the empty space below the mural had become a gathering spot. At least until the new condos would tower over Leon.

"They can try and get rid of us, but part of us will always be there," Mama B said when Kayla had one of the shelter workers, the one who believed everything was reparable, take the picture. "And we'll be there for each other because we are what we have."

"*K^{w}u mrímstn.*" Gloria knew how to say the words.

Along with that testament to family, and snapshots from the party, Kayla kept three more photographs inside.

One was of an alley where a tent had once been, its welcome mat always ghostily present.

One was of stains on the sidewalk like stories.

And one image she had brought for herself and had also left for Little Zoe: a rusted sewer grate where a yellow flower had once bloomed, and might one day bloom bright again.

Was always blooming.

Approaching Dawn

The walk from Leon Avenue was long. Her heart felt full from the celebration with her friends the night before. She could also feel the journey's distance in her bad leg. But the grasses and wildflowers along the roadside were alive with crickets, and the light dim but becoming enough to see by.

Livia had offered to drive her, and she knew Ketchum would have walked her there. But she needed to get there by herself.

And she brought with her the memories of what she could not and would not leave behind. Memories of the night she'd fled with blood on her hands, of the brown and orange plaid couch, of the men she'd gone with to convince herself she was beyond feeling. They were there but would not prevent her from seeing more, being more.

She also brought, inside her, the chestnut she had planted and watered as a child, the love she had for *t'st'siɬp,* the gift of the yellow flower Little Zoe shown her.

She had wondered if she was so broken that there was nothing left to break. But she was still here. She was still walking, alone but not alone.

She took in the trees, the tangles of wildflowers as the sky brightened, the crickets and the wind, the mountains and the lake, at once so dark in its depths yet also gleaming with first promise of sunlight.

She took a picture so she would always have this.

She walked past orchards with cherry trees blooming, past apple and peach in leaf, past pines and spruce and glimmers of the water possible through the trees. Past deer grazing on a hill, birds gathering in the branches. Past houses with the first rectangles of light starting to appear.

And there it was: a small farm, paddocks with early summer grass emerging, run-in sheds for bad weather, a barn at the end of a long drive. It was a farm Demi Ray had told her about, one she had walked by once on Lakeshore.

As she approached, she could smell the fresh-cut hay and the horses, even from the road.

She would not be able to ride again, but simply being around the horses would be enough. Even knowing they were there. And her hands knew work.

She breathed the scents in like a memory coming back to life. But it was more than a memory. It was a new gift. One she was giving herself.

There was a light on in the barn. She walked forwards, listening to the sound of her own footsteps. She took in the smell of the barn and the horses and the chill morning air, breathing in deeply and at last.

And it was beautiful, still.

Acknowledgements

Many thanks to the dear friends and family who have provided invaluable insights, support, and belief in this book: Michelle Soucie, Tricia McCraney, Shawneen Jacobs, Munira Hussein, Hannah Minett, Julie Garner, Sakiru Adebayo, Jennifer Gustar, Ozma Masood, and Leslie Cockerline.

I am always incredibly grateful for George Grinnell and Sam Grinnell for all our conversations, all you have helped this book become, and, most of all, for being there with all your love. I could not have done this journey without you. Here's to many more.

Tremendous thanks to Jeremy Luke Hill of The Porcupine's Quill, for your insight and vision, and your commitment to Canadian publishing. Thank you to Mary Hamilton for your fantastic copy editing. Lim lemt to Syilx Knowledge Keeper Jasmine Peone, for your wisdom and so generously sharing Nsyilxcn language and Syilx culture, and to Syilx Elders Pamela Barnes and Grouse Barnes for sharing your insights. Lim lemt to Syilx (Okanagan) artist Sheldon Pierre Louis for allowing me to share your mural on Leon Avenue, "*k*^{w}*u mrímstn*". Honour and gratitude to the Syilx Okanagan people on whose unceded, ancestral, and traditional land I am an uninvited and grateful guest. To Janine Little, believer in 200%; to Kelsey, Jane, and Bruce for being there; to my late aunt, Lois Ann Rovira, for your love, encouragement, and kindred spirit; to Peter Carey, for your excellent teachings; to Deni Béchard; and to those who know or knew these streets—or the new places you find yourself—for your wisdom, courage, and friendship.

About the Author

Joanna Cockerline is a CBC Literary Awards prizewinner who has been published in national and international journals and magazines such as *Room, The Fiddlehead, En Route,* and *International Human Rights Arts.* She was nominated for the Pushcart Prize in 2022.

Joanna earned her BA and MA in English Literature at the University of Guelph and completed a graduate program at the Humber School for Writers with two-time Booker Prize winner Peter Carey.

She co-authored the short story collection *Seeing Our Sisters* alongside Kenyan authors in The Girlship Collective in 2024. She is actively at work on her next novel.

A long-time street outreach volunteer with an organization that won the City of Kelowna Volunteer Organization of the Year Award, Joanna has recently co-founded a non-profit organization dedicated to the unhoused community and, particularly, street-level sex workers.

Joanna lives with her family in the traditional, ancestral, and unceded Syilx Okanagan Territory of Kelowna, BC, where she teaches literature and creative writing at the University of British Columbia (UBC) Okanagan.